P9-AFM-979

EXTRAORDINARY INTERNATIONAL PRAISE FOR

THE OCEAN AT THE END OF THE LANE

"His prose is simple but poetic, his world strange but utterly believable—if he was South American we would call this magic realism rather than fantasy."

The Times (London)

"Gaiman lets his narrator share his memories with curious incredulousness and incredible calm. That allows the story to wash over readers, to overwhelm us slowly and deliciously. We're invited into the mist too, and it's a squirmy thing."

Savannah Morning News

"[Gaiman] paints a child's life with wrenching sympathy and precision, and delivers an engrossing myth for our age. *The Ocean at the End of the Lane*, full of discovery and bonding, sacrifice and heroism, will gratify Gaiman fans and new readers alike."

Columbus Dispatch

"Worthy of a sleepless night . . . a fairy tale for adults that explores both innocence lost and the enthusiasm for seeing what's past one's proverbial fence . . . Gaiman is a master of creating worlds just a step to the left of our own."

USA Today

"Mr. Gaiman labels *The Ocean at the End of the Lane* 'for all ages,' which is exactly right. It has grief, fear and regret, as well as love and awe—adult emotions, but children feel them too. The best fantasy keeps its feet firmly planted in the real world while offering a vision of what lies beyond, and like all Mr. Gaiman's work, this is fantasy of the very best."

Wall Street Journal

"Poignant and heartbreaking, eloquent and frightening, impeccably rendered, it's a fable that reminds us how our lives are shaped by childhood experiences, what we gain from them and the price we pay."

Kirkus Reviews (★ starred review ★)

"Remarkable . . . wrenchingly, gorgeously elegiac. . . . [I]n *The Ocean at the End of the Lane*, [Gaiman] summons up childhood magic and adventure while acknowledging their irrevocable loss, and he stitches the elegiac contradictions together so tightly that you won't see the seams."

Minneapolis Star Tribune

"[A] compelling tale for all ages . . . entirely absorbing and wholly moving."

New York *Daily News*

"[A] story concerning the bewildering gulf between the innocent and the authoritative, the powerless and the powerful, the child and the adult. . . . *Ocean* is a novel to approach without caution; the author is clearly operating at the height of his career."

The Atlantic Wire

"*Ocean* has that nearly invisible prose that keeps the focus firmly on the storytelling, and not on the writing. . . . This simple exterior hides something much more interesting; in the same way that what looks like a pond can really be an ocean."

io9

"A terrifying shift in the nature of things lies at the heart of Neil Gaimain's rich new novel."

The Guardian

"In Gaiman's latest romp through otherworldly adventure, a young boy discovers a neighboring family's supernatural secret. Soon his innocence is tested by ancient, magical forces, and he learns the power of true friendship. The result is a captivating read, equal parts sweet, sad, and spooky."

Parade

"*The Ocean at the End of the Lane* is fun to read, filled with his trademarked blend of sinister whimsy. Gaiman's writing is like dangerous candy—you're certain there's ground glass somewhere, but it just tastes so good!"

Bookish *(Houston Chronicle* book blog*)*

"The impotence of childhood is often the first thing sentimental adults forget about it; Gaiman is able to resurrect, with brutal immediacy, the abject misery of being unable to control one's own life."

Laura Miller, *Salon*

"Wry and freaky and finally sad. . . . This is how Gaiman works his charms. . . . He crafts his stories with one eye on the old world, on Irish folktales and Robin Hood and Camelot, and the other on particle physics and dark matter."

Chicago Tribune

"Gaiman has crafted an achingly beautiful memoir of an imagination and a spellbinding story that sets three women at the center of everything. . . . It's a meditation on memory and mortality, a creative reflection on how the defining moments of childhood can inhabit the worlds we imagine."

Milwaukee Journal Sentinel

"This slim novel, gorgeously written, keeps its talons in you long after you've finished."

New York Post

"Reading Gaiman's new novel, his first for adults since 2005's *The Anansi Boys*, is like listening to that rare friend whose dreams you actually want to hear about at breakfast. . . . Gaiman's at his fantasy-master best here—the struggle between a boy and a shape shifter with 'rotting-cloth eyes' moves at a speedy, chilling clip. What distinguishes the book, though, is its evocation of the powerlessness and wonder of childhood, a time when magic seems as likely as any other answer and good stories help us through."

People

Also by Neil Gaiman

THE
OCEAN AT
THE END OF
THE LANE

A Novel

NEIL
GAIMAN

HARPER

An Imprint of HarperCollinsPublishers

Grateful acknowledgment is given to Art Spiegelman for permission to use a word balloon from his collaborative conversation with Maurice Sendak in *The New Yorker*, copyright © by Art Spiegelman. All rights reserved.

HARPER

An Imprint of HarperCollins*Publishers*
195 Broadway,
New York, New York 10007.

Copyright © 2013 by Neil Gaiman
ISBN 978-0-06-232513-6

First Harper mass market international printing: April 2014
First William Morrow hardcover printing: June 2013

HarperCollins® and Harper® are registered trademarks of HarperCollins Publishers.

Printed in the United States of America

Visit Harper paperbacks on the World Wide Web at
www.harpercollins.com

10 9 8 7 6 5 4 3 2

For Amanda,
who wanted to know

"*I remember my own childhood vividly . . . I knew terrible things. But I knew I mustn't let adults know I knew. It would scare them.*"

MAURICE SENDAK, IN CONVERSATION WITH ART SPIEGELMAN,

THE NEW YORKER, SEPTEMBER 27, 1993

It was only a duck pond, out at the back of the farm. It wasn't very big.

Lettie Hempstock said it was an ocean, but I knew that was silly. She said they'd come here across the ocean from the old country.

Her mother said that Lettie didn't remember properly, and it was a long time ago, and anyway, the old country had sunk.

Old Mrs. Hempstock, Lettie's grandmother, said they were both wrong, and that the place that had sunk wasn't the *really* old country. She said she could remember the really old country.

She said the really old country had blown up.

Prologue

I wore a black suit and a white shirt, a black tie and black shoes, all polished and shiny: clothes that normally would make me feel uncomfortable, as if I were in a stolen uniform, or pretending to be an adult. Today they gave me comfort of a kind. I was wearing the right clothes for a hard day.

I had done my duty in the morning, spoken the words I was meant to speak, and I meant them as I spoke them, and then, when the service was done, I got in my car and I drove, randomly, without a plan, with an hour or so to kill before I met more people I had not seen for years and shook more hands and drank too many cups of tea from the best china. I drove along winding Sussex country roads I only half-remembered, until I found myself headed toward the town center, so I turned, randomly, down another road, and took a left, and a right. It was only then that I realized where I was going, where I had been going all along, and I grimaced at my own foolishness.

I had been driving toward a house that had not existed for decades.

I thought of turning around, then, as I drove down a wide street that had once been a flint lane beside a barley field, of turning back and leaving the past undisturbed. But I was curious.

The old house, the one I had lived in for seven years, from when I was five until I was twelve, that house had been knocked down and was lost for good. The new house, the one my parents had built at the bottom of the garden, between the azalea bushes and the green circle in the grass we called the fairy ring, that had been sold thirty years ago.

I slowed the car as I saw the new house. It would always be the new house in my head. I pulled up into the driveway, observing the way they had built out on the mid-seventies architecture. I had forgotten that the bricks of the house were chocolate-brown. The new people had made my mother's tiny balcony into a two-story sunroom. I stared at the house, remembering less than I had expected about my teenage years: no good times, no bad times. I'd lived in that place, for a while, as a teenager. It didn't seem to be any part of who I was now.

I backed the car out of their driveway.

It was time, I knew, to drive to my sister's bustling, cheerful house, all tidied and stiff for the day. I would talk to people whose existence I had forgotten years before and they would ask me about my marriage (failed a decade ago, a relationship that had slowly frayed until eventually, as they always seem to, it broke) and whether I was seeing anyone (I wasn't; I was not even sure that I could, not yet) and they would ask about my children (all grown up, they have their own lives, they wish they could be here today), work (doing fine, thank you, I would say, never knowing how to talk about what I do. If I could talk about it, I would not have to do it. I make art, sometimes I make true art, and sometimes it fills the empty places in my life. Some of them. Not all). We would talk about the departed; we would remember the dead.

The little country lane of my childhood had become a black tarmac road that served as a buffer between two sprawling housing estates. I drove further down it, away from the town, which was not the way I should have been traveling, and it felt good.

The slick black road became narrower, windier, became the single-lane track I remembered from my childhood, became packed earth and knobbly, bone-like flints.

Soon I was driving, slowly, bumpily, down a narrow lane with brambles and briar roses on each side, wherever the edge was not a stand of hazels or a wild hedgerow. It felt like I had driven back in time. That lane was how I remembered it, when nothing else was.

I drove past Caraway Farm. I remembered being just-sixteen, and kissing red-cheeked, fair-haired Callie Anders, who lived there, and whose family would soon move to the Shetlands, and I would never kiss her or see her again. Then nothing but fields on either side of the road, for almost a mile: a tangle of meadows. Slowly the lane became a track. It was reaching its end.

I remembered it before I turned the corner and saw it, in all its dilapidated red-brick glory: the Hempstocks' farmhouse.

It took me by surprise, although that was where the lane had always ended. I could have gone no further. I parked the car at the side of the farmyard. I had no plan. I wondered whether, after all these years, there was anyone still living there, or, more precisely, if the Hempstocks were still living there. It seemed unlikely, but then, from what little I remembered, they had been unlikely people.

The stench of cow muck struck me as I got out of the car, and I walked, gingerly, across the small yard to the front door. I looked for a doorbell, in vain, and then I knocked. The door had not been latched properly, and it swung gently open as I rapped it with my knuckles.

I had been here, hadn't I, a long time ago? I was sure I had. Childhood memories are sometimes covered and obscured beneath the things that come later, like childhood toys forgotten at the bottom of a crammed adult closet, but they are never lost for good. I stood in the hallway and called, "Hello? Is there anybody here?"

I heard nothing. I smelled bread-baking and wax furniture polish and old wood. My eyes were slow to adjust to the darkness: I peered into it, was getting ready to turn and leave when an elderly woman came out of the dim hallway holding a white duster. She wore her gray hair long.

I said, "Mrs. Hempstock?"

She tipped her head to one side, looked at me. "Yes. I *do* know you, young man," she said. I am not a young man. Not any longer. "I know you, but things get messy when you get to my age. Who are you, exactly?"

"I think I must have been about seven, maybe eight, the last time I was here."

She smiled then. "You were Lettie's friend? From the top of the lane?"

"You gave me milk. It was warm, from the cows." And then I realized how many years had gone by, and I said, "No, you didn't do that, that must have been your mother who gave me the milk. I'm sorry." As we age, we become our parents; live long enough and we see faces repeat in time. I remembered Mrs. Hempstock, Lettie's mother, as a stout woman. This woman was stick-thin, and she looked delicate. She looked like her mother, like the woman I had known as Old Mrs. Hempstock.

Sometimes when I look in the mirror I see my father's face, not my own, and I remember the way he would smile at himself, in mirrors, before he went out. "Looking good," he'd say to his reflection, approvingly. "Looking good."

"Are you here to see Lettie?" Mrs. Hempstock asked.

"Is she here?" The idea surprised me. She had *gone* somewhere, hadn't she? America?

The old woman shook her head. "I was just about to put the kettle on. Do you fancy a spot of tea?"

I hesitated. Then I said that, if she didn't mind, I'd like it if she could point me toward the duck pond first.

"Duck pond?"

I knew Lettie had had a funny name for it. I remembered that. "She called it the sea. Something like that."

The old woman put the cloth down on the dresser. "Can't drink the water from the sea, can you? Too salty. Like drinking life's blood. Do you remember the way? You can get to it around the side of the house. Just follow the path."

If you'd asked me an hour before, I would have said no, I did not remember the way. I do not even think I would have remembered Lettie Hempstock's name. But standing in that hallway, it was all coming back to me. Memories were waiting at the edges of things, beckoning to me. Had you told me that I was seven again, I might have half-believed you, for a moment.

"Thank you."

I walked into the farmyard. I went past the chicken coop, past the old barn and along the edge of the field, remembering where I was, and what was coming next, and exulting in the knowledge. Hazels lined the side of the meadow. I picked a handful of the green nuts, put them in my pocket.

The pond is next, I thought. *I just have to go around this shed, and I'll see it.*

I saw it and felt oddly proud of myself, as if that one act of memory had blown away some of the cobwebs of the day.

The pond was smaller than I remembered. There was a little wooden shed on the far side, and, by the path, an ancient, heavy, wood-and-metal bench. The peeling wooden slats had been painted green a few years ago. I sat on the bench, and stared at the reflection of the sky in the water, at the scum of duckweed at the edges, and the half-dozen lily pads. Every now and again, I tossed a hazelnut into the middle of the pond, the pond that Lettie Hempstock had called . . .

It wasn't the sea, was it?

She would be older than I am now, Lettie Hempstock. She was only a handful of years older than I was back then, for all her funny talk. She was eleven. I was . . . what was I? It was after the bad birthday party. I knew that. So I would have been seven.

I wondered if we had ever fallen in the water. Had I pushed her into the duck pond, that strange girl who lived in the farm at the very bottom of the lane? I remembered her being in the water. Perhaps she had pushed me in too.

Where did she go? America? No, *Australia*. That was it. Somewhere a long way away.

And it wasn't the sea. It was the ocean.

Lettie Hempstock's ocean.

I remembered that, and, remembering that, I remembered everything.

I.

Nobody came to my seventh birthday party.

There was a table laid with jellies and trifles, with a party hat beside each place, and a birthday cake with seven candles on it in the center of the table. The cake had a book drawn on it, in icing. My mother, who had organized the party, told me that the lady at the bakery said that they had never put a book on a birthday cake before, and that mostly for boys it was footballs or spaceships. I was their first book.

When it became obvious that nobody was coming, my mother lit the seven candles on the cake, and I blew them out. I ate a slice of the cake, as did my little sister and one of her friends (both of them attending the party as observers, not participants) before they fled, giggling, to the garden.

Party games had been prepared by my mother but, because nobody was there, not even my sister, none of the party games were played, and I unwrapped the newspaper around the pass-the-parcel gift myself, revealing a blue plastic Batman figure. I was sad that nobody had come to my party, but happy that I had a Batman figure, and there was a birthday present waiting to be read, a boxed set of the Narnia books, which I took upstairs. I lay on the bed and lost myself in the stories.

I liked that. Books were safer than other people anyway.

My parents had also given me a *Best of Gilbert and Sullivan* LP, to add to the two that I already had. I had loved Gilbert and Sullivan since I was three, when my father's youngest sister, my aunt, took me to see *Iolanthe*, a play filled with lords and fairies. I found the existence and nature of the fairies easier to understand than that of the lords. My aunt had died soon after, of pneumonia, in the hospital.

That evening my father arrived home from work and he brought a cardboard box with him. In the cardboard box was a soft-haired black kitten of uncertain gender, whom I immediately named Fluffy, and which I loved utterly and wholeheartedly.

Fluffy slept on my bed at night. I talked to it, sometimes, when my little sister was not around, half-expecting it to answer in a human tongue. It never did. I did not mind. The kitten was affectionate and interested and a good companion for someone whose seventh birthday party had consisted of a table with iced biscuits and a blancmange and cake and fifteen empty folding chairs.

I do not remember ever asking any of the other children in my class at school why they had not come to my party. I did not need to ask them. They were not my friends, after all. They were just the people I went to school with.

I made friends slowly, when I made them.

I had books, and now I had my kitten. We would be like Dick Whittington and his cat, I knew, or, if Fluffy proved particularly intelligent, we would be the miller's son and Puss-in-Boots. The kitten slept on my pillow, and it even waited for me to come home from school, sitting on the driveway in front of my house, by the fence, until, a month later, it was run over by the taxi that brought the opal miner to stay at my house.

I was not there when it happened.

I got home from school that day, and my kitten was not waiting to meet me. In the kitchen was a tall, rangy man with tanned skin and a checked shirt. He was drinking coffee at the kitchen table, I could smell it. In those days all coffee was instant coffee, a bitter dark brown powder that came out of a jar.

"I'm afraid I had a little accident arriving here," he told me, cheerfully. "But not to worry." His accent was clipped, unfamiliar: it was the first South African accent I had heard.

He, too, had a cardboard box on the table in front of him.

"The black kitten, was he yours?" he asked.

"It's called Fluffy," I said.

"Yeah. Like I said. Accident coming here. Not to worry. Disposed of the corpse. Don't have to trouble yourself. Dealt with the matter. Open the box."

"What?"

He pointed to the box. "Open it," he said.

The opal miner was a tall man. He wore jeans and checked shirts every time I saw him, except the last. He had a thick chain of pale gold around his neck. That was gone the last time I saw him, too.

I did not want to open his box. I wanted to go off on my own. I wanted to cry for my kitten, but I could not do that if anyone else was there and watching me. I wanted to mourn. I wanted to bury my friend at the bottom of the garden, past the green-grass fairy ring, into the rhododendron bush cave, back past the heap of grass cuttings, where nobody ever went but me.

The box moved.

"Bought it for you," said the man. "Always pay my debts."

I reached out, lifted the top flap of the box, wondering if this was a joke, if my kitten would be in there. Instead a ginger face stared up at me truculently.

The opal miner took the cat out of the box.

He was a huge, ginger-striped tomcat, missing half an ear. He glared at me angrily. This cat had not liked being put in a box. He was not used to boxes. I reached out to stroke his head, feeling unfaithful to the memory of my kitten, but he pulled back so I could not touch him, and he hissed at me, then stalked off to a far corner of the room, where he sat and looked and hated.

"There you go. Cat for a cat," said the opal miner, and he ruffled my hair with his leathery hand. Then he went out into the hall, leaving me in the kitchen with the cat that was not my kitten.

The man put his head back through the door. "He's called Monster," he said.

It felt like a bad joke.

I propped open the kitchen door, so the cat could get out. Then I went up to the bedroom, and lay on my bed, and cried for dead Fluffy. When my parents got home that evening, I do not think my kitten was even mentioned.

Monster lived with us for a week or more. I put cat food in the bowl for him in the morning and again at night as I had for my kitten. He would sit by the back door until I, or someone else, let him out. We saw him in the garden, slipping from bush to bush, or in trees, or in the undergrowth. We could trace his movements by the dead blue-tits and thrushes we would find in the garden, but we saw him rarely.

I missed Fluffy. I knew you could not simply replace something alive, but I dared not grumble to my parents about it. They would have been baffled at my upset: after all, if my kitten had been killed, it had also been replaced. The damage had been made up.

It all came back and even as it came back I knew it would not be for long: all the things I remembered, sitting on the green bench beside the little pond that Lettie Hempstock had once convinced me was an ocean.

II.

I was not happy as a child, although from time to time I was content. I lived in books more than I lived anywhere else.

Our house was large and many-roomed, which was good when they bought it and my father had money, not good later.

My parents called me into their bedroom one afternoon, very formally. I thought I must have done something wrong and was there for a telling-off, but no: they told me only that they were no longer affluent, that we would all need to make sacrifices, and that what I would be sacrificing was my bedroom, the little room at the top of the stairs. I was sad: my bedroom had a tiny little yellow washbasin they had put in for me, just my size; the room was above the kitchen, and immediately up the stairs from the television room, so at night I could hear the comforting buzz of adult conversation coming from below, through my half-open door, and I did not feel alone. Also, in my bedroom, nobody minded if I kept the hall door half-open, allowing in enough light that I was not scared of the dark, and, just as important, allowing me to read secretly, after my bedtime, using the dim hallway light to read by, if I needed to. I always needed to.

Exiled to my little sister's huge bedroom, I was not heartbroken. There were already three beds in there, and I took the bed by the window. I loved that I could climb out of that bedroom window onto the long brick balcony, that I could sleep with my window open and feel the wind and the rain on my face. But we argued, my sister and

I, argued about everything. She liked to sleep with the door to the hall closed, and the immediate arguments about whether the bedroom door should be open or shut were summarily resolved by my mother writing a chart that hung on the back of the door, showing that alternate nights were mine or my sister's. Each night I was content or I was terrified, depending on whether the door was open or closed.

My former bedroom at the top of the stairs was let out, and a variety of people passed through it. I viewed them all with suspicion: they were sleeping in my bedroom, using my little yellow basin that was just the right size for me. There had been a fat Austrian lady who told us she could leave her head and walk around the ceiling; an architectural student from New Zealand; an American couple whom my mother, scandalized, made leave when she discovered they were not actually married; and, now, there was the opal miner.

He was a South African, although he had made his money mining for opals in Australia. He gave my sister and me an opal each, a rough black rock with green-blue-red fire in it. My sister liked him for this, and treasured her opal stone. I could not forgive him for the death of my kitten.

It was the first day of the spring holidays: three weeks of no school. I woke early, thrilled by the prospect of endless days to fill however I wished. I would read. I would explore.

I pulled on my shorts, my T-shirt, my sandals. I went downstairs to the kitchen. My father was cooking, while my mother slept in. He was wearing his dressing gown over his pajamas. He often cooked breakfast on Saturdays. I said, "Dad! Where's my comic?" He always bought me a copy of SMASH! before he drove home from work on Fridays, and I would read it on Saturday mornings.

"In the back of the car. Do you want toast?"

"Yes," I said. "But not burnt."

My father did not like toasters. He toasted bread under the grill, and, usually, he burnt it.

I went outside into the drive. I looked around. I went back into the house, pushed the kitchen door, went in. I liked the kitchen door. It swung both ways, in and out, so servants sixty years ago would be able to walk in or out with their arms laden with dishes empty or full.

"Dad? Where's the car?"

"In the drive."

"No, it isn't."

"*What?*"

The telephone rang, and my father went out into the hall, where the phone was, to answer it. I heard him talking to someone.

The toast began to smoke under the grill.

I got up on a chair and turned the grill off.

"That was the police," my father said. "Someone's reported seeing our car abandoned at the bottom of the lane. I said I hadn't even reported it stolen yet. Right. We can head down now, meet them there. *Toast!*"

He pulled the pan out from beneath the grill. The toast was smoking and blackened on one side.

"Is my comic there? Or did they steal it?"

"I don't know. The police didn't mention your comic."

My father put peanut butter on the burnt side of each piece of toast, replaced his dressing gown with a coat worn over his pajamas, put on a pair of shoes, and we walked down the lane together. He munched his toast as we walked. I held my toast, and did not eat it.

We had walked for perhaps five minutes down the narrow lane which ran through fields on each side, when a police car came up behind us. It slowed, and the driver greeted my father by name.

I hid my piece of burnt toast behind my back while my father talked to the policeman. I wished my family would buy normal sliced white bread, the kind that went into toasters, like every other family I knew. My father had found a local baker's shop where they made thick loaves of heavy brown bread, and he insisted on buying them. He said they tasted better, which was, to my mind, nonsense. Proper bread was white, and pre-sliced, and tasted like almost nothing: that was the point.

The driver of the police car got out, opened the passenger door, told me to get in. My father rode up front beside the driver.

The police car went slowly down the lane. The whole lane was unpaved back then, just wide enough for one car at a time, a puddly, precipitous, bumpy way, with flints sticking up from it, the whole thing rutted by farm equipment and rain and time.

"These kids," said the policeman. "They think it's funny. Steal a car, drive it around, abandon it. They'll be locals."

"I'm just glad it was found so fast," said my father.

Past Caraway Farm, where a small girl with hair so blonde it was almost white, and red, red cheeks, stared at us as we went past. I held my piece of burnt toast on my lap.

"Funny them leaving it down here, though," said the policeman, "because it's a long walk back to anywhere from here."

We passed a bend in the lane and saw the white Mini over on the side, in front of a gate leading into a field, tires sunk deep in the brown mud. We drove past it, parked on the grass verge. The policeman let me out, and the three of us walked over to the Mini, while the policeman told my dad about crime in this area, and why it was obviously the local kids had done it, then my dad was opening the passenger side door with his spare key.

He said, "Someone left something on the back seat." My father reached back and pulled the blue blanket away, that covered the thing in the back seat, even as the policeman was telling him that he shouldn't do that, and I was staring at the back seat because that was where my comic was, so I saw it.

It was an *it*, the thing I was looking at, not a *him*.

Although I was an imaginative child, prone to nightmares, I had persuaded my parents to take me to Madame Tussauds waxworks in London, when I was six, because I had wanted to visit the Chamber of Horrors, expecting the movie-monster Chambers of Horrors I'd read about in my comics. I had wanted to thrill to waxworks of Dracula and Frankenstein's Monster and the Wolf-man. Instead I was walked through a seemingly endless sequence of dioramas of unremarkable, glum-looking men and women who had murdered people—usually lodgers, and members of their own families—and who were then murdered in their turn: by hanging, by the electric chair, in gas chambers. Most of them were depicted with their victims in awkward, social situations—seated around a dinner table, perhaps, as their poisoned family members expired. The plaques that explained who they were also told me that the majority of them had murdered their families and sold the bodies to *anatomy*. It was then that the word *anatomy* garnered its own edge of horror for me. I did not know what *anatomy* was. I knew only that *anatomy* made people kill their children.

The only thing that had kept me from running screaming from the Chamber of Horrors as I was led around it was that none of the waxworks had looked fully convincing. They could not truly look dead, because they did not ever look alive.

The thing in the back seat that had been covered by the blue blanket (I *knew* that blanket. It was the one that had been in my old bedroom, on the shelf, for when it got cold) was not convincing either. It looked a little like the opal miner, but it was dressed in a black suit, with a white, ruffled shirt and a black bow-tie. Its hair was slicked back and artificially shiny. Its eyes were staring. Its lips were bluish, but its skin was very red. It looked like a parody of health. There was no gold chain around its neck.

I could see, underneath it, crumpled and bent, my copy of SMASH! with Batman, looking just as he did on the television, on the cover.

I don't remember who said what then, just that they made me stand away from the Mini. I crossed the road, and I stood there on my own while the policeman talked to my father and wrote things down in a notebook.

I stared at the Mini. A length of green garden hose ran from the exhaust pipe up to the driver's window. There was thick brown mud all over the exhaust, holding the hosepipe in place.

Nobody was watching me. I took a bite of my toast. It was burnt and cold.

At home, my father ate all the most burnt pieces of toast. "Yum!" he'd say, and "Charcoal! Good for you!" and "Burnt toast! My favorite!" and he'd eat it all up. When I was much older he confessed to me that he had not ever liked burnt toast, had only eaten it to prevent it from going to waste, and, for a fraction of a moment, my entire childhood felt like a lie: it was as if one of the pillars of belief that my world had been built upon had crumbled into dry sand.

The policeman spoke into a radio in the front of his car.

Then he crossed the road and came over to me. "Sorry about this, sonny," he said. "There's going to be a few more cars coming down this road in a minute. We should find you somewhere to wait that you won't be in the way. Would you like to sit in the back of my car again?"

I shook my head. I didn't want to sit there again.

Somebody, a girl, said, "He can come back with me to the farmhouse. It's no trouble."

She was much older than me, at least eleven. Her red-brown hair was worn relatively short, for a girl, and her nose was snub. She was freckled. She wore a red skirt—girls didn't wear jeans much back then, not in those parts. She had a soft Sussex accent and sharp gray-blue eyes.

The girl went, with the policeman, over to my father, and she got permission to take me away, and then I was walking down the lane with her.

I said, "There is a dead man in our car."

"That's why he came down here," she told me. "The end of the road. Nobody's going to find him and stop him around here, three o'clock in the morning. And the mud there is wet and easy to mold."

"Do you think he killed himself?"

"Yes. Do you like milk? Gran's milking Bessie now."

I said, "You mean, real milk from a cow?" and then felt foolish, but she nodded, reassuringly.

I thought about this. I'd never had milk that didn't come from a bottle. "I think I'd like that."

We stopped at a small barn where an old woman, much older than my parents, with long gray hair, like cobwebs, and a thin face, was standing beside a cow. Long black tubes were attached to each of the cow's teats. "We used to milk them by hand," she told me. "But this is easier."

She showed me how the milk went from the cow down the black tubes and into the machine, through a cooler and into huge metal churns. The churns were left on a heavy wooden platform outside the barn, where they would be collected each day by a lorry.

The old lady gave me a cup of creamy milk from Bessie the cow, the fresh milk before it had gone through the cooler. Nothing I had drunk had ever tasted like that before: rich and warm and perfectly happy in my mouth. I remembered that milk after I had forgotten everything else.

"There's more of them up the lane," said the old woman, suddenly. "All sorts coming down with lights flashing and all. Such a palaver. You should get the boy into the kitchen. He's hungry, and a cup of milk won't do a growing boy."

The girl said, "Have you eaten?"

"Just a piece of toast. It was burned."

She said, "My name's Lettie. Lettie Hempstock. This is Hempstock Farm. Come on." She took me in through the front door, and into their enormous kitchen, sat me down at a huge wooden table, so stained and patterned that it looked as if faces were staring up at me from the old wood.

"We have breakfast here early," she said. "Milking starts at first light. But there's porridge in the saucepan, and jam to put in it."

She gave me a china bowl filled with warm porridge from the stovetop, with a lump of homemade blackberry jam, my favorite, in the middle of the porridge, then she poured cream on it. I swished it around with my spoon before I ate it, swirling it into a purple mess, and was as happy as I have ever been about anything. It tasted perfect.

A stocky woman came in. Her red-brown hair was streaked with gray, and cut short. She had apple cheeks, a dark green skirt that went to her knees, and Wellington boots. She said, "This must be the boy from the top of the lane. Such a business going on with that car. There'll be five of them needing tea soon."

Lettie filled a huge copper kettle from the tap. She lit a gas hob with a match and put the kettle onto the flame. Then she took down five chipped mugs from a cupboard, and hesitated, looking at the woman. The woman said, "You're right. Six. The doctor will be here too."

Then the woman pursed her lips and made a *tchutch!* noise. "They've missed the note," she said. "He wrote it so carefully too, folded it and put it in his breast pocket, and they haven't looked there yet."

"What does it say?" asked Lettie.

"Read it yourself," said the woman. I thought she was Lettie's mother. She seemed like she was somebody's mother. Then she said, "It says that he took all the money that his friends had given him to smuggle out of South Africa and bank for them in England, along with all the money he'd made over the years mining for opals, and he went to the casino in Brighton, to gamble, but he only meant to gamble with his own money. And then he only meant to dip into the money his friends had given him until he had made back the money he had lost.

"And then he didn't have anything," said the woman, "and all was dark."

"That's not what he wrote, though," said Lettie, squinting her eyes. "What he wrote was,

"*To all my friends,*

"*Am so sorry it was not like I meant to and hope you can find it in your hearts to forgive me for I cannot forgive myself.*"

"Same thing," said the older woman. She turned to me. "I'm Lettie's ma," she said. "You'll have met my mother already, in the milking shed. I'm Mrs. Hempstock, but she was Mrs. Hempstock before me, so she's Old Mrs. Hempstock. This is Hempstock Farm. It's the oldest farm hereabouts. It's in the Domesday Book."

I wondered why they were all called Hempstock, those women,

but I did not ask, any more than I dared to ask how they knew about the suicide note or what the opal miner had thought as he died. They were perfectly matter-of-fact about it.

Lettie said, "I nudged him to look in the breast pocket. He'll think he thought of it himself."

"There's a good girl," said Mrs. Hempstock. "They'll be in here when the kettle boils to ask if I've seen anything unusual and to have their tea. Why don't you take the boy down to the pond?"

"It's not a pond," said Lettie. "It's my ocean." She turned to me and said, "Come on." She led me out of the house the way we had come.

The day was still gray.

We walked around the house, down the cow path.

"Is it a real ocean?" I asked.

"Oh yes," she said.

We came on it suddenly: a wooden shed, an old bench, and between them, a duck pond, dark water spotted with duckweed and lily pads. There was a dead fish, silver as a coin, floating on its side on the surface.

"That's not good," said Lettie.

"I thought you said it was an ocean," I told her. "It's just a pond, really."

"It *is* an ocean," she said. "We came across it when I was just a baby, from the old country."

Lettie went into the shed and came out with a long bamboo pole, with what looked like a shrimping net on the end. She leaned over, carefully pushed the net beneath the dead fish. She pulled it out.

"But Hempstock Farm is in the Domesday Book," I said. "Your mum said so. And that was William the Conqueror."

"Yes," said Lettie Hempstock.

She took the dead fish out of the net and examined it. It was still soft, not stiff, and it flopped in her hand. I had never seen so many colors: it was silver, yes, but beneath the silver was blue and green and purple and each scale was tipped with black.

"What kind of fish is it?" I asked.

"This is very odd," she said. "I mean, mostly fish in this ocean don't die anyway." She produced a horn-handled pocketknife, although I could not have told you from where, and she pushed it into the stomach of the fish, and sliced along, toward the tail.

"This is what killed her," said Lettie.

She took something from inside the fish. Then she put it, still greasy from the fish-guts, into my hand. I bent down, dipped it into the water, rubbed my fingers across it to clean it off. I stared at it. Queen Victoria's face stared back at me.

"Sixpence?" I said. "The fish ate a sixpence?"

"It's not good, is it?" said Lettie Hempstock. There was a little sunshine now: it showed the freckles that clustered across her cheeks and nose, and, where the sunlight touched her hair, it was a coppery red. And then she said, "Your father's wondering where you are. Time to be getting back."

I tried to give her the little silver sixpence, but she shook her head. "You keep it," she said. "You can buy chocolates, or sherbet lemons."

"I don't think I can," I said. "It's too small. I don't know if shops will take sixpences like these nowadays."

"Then put it in your piggy bank," she said. "It might bring you luck." She said this doubtfully, as if she were uncertain what kind of luck it would bring.

The policeman and my father and two men in brown suits and ties were standing in the farmhouse kitchen. One of the men told me he was a policeman, but he wasn't wearing a uniform, which I thought was disappointing: if I were a policeman, I was certain, I would wear my uniform whenever I could. The other man with a suit and tie I recognized as Doctor Smithson, our family doctor. They were finishing their tea.

My father thanked Mrs. Hempstock and Lettie for taking care of me, and they said I was no trouble at all, and that I could come again. The policeman who had driven us down to the Mini now drove us back to our house, and dropped us off at the end of the drive.

"Probably best if you don't talk about this to your sister," said my father.

I didn't want to talk about it to anybody. I had found a special place, and made a new friend, and lost my comic, and I was holding an old-fashioned silver sixpence tightly in my hand.

I said, "What makes the ocean different to the sea?"

"Bigger," said my father. "An ocean is much bigger than the sea. Why?"

"Just thinking," I said. "Could you have an ocean that was as small as a pond?"

"No," said my father. "Ponds are pond-sized, lakes are lake-sized. Seas are seas and oceans are oceans. Atlantic, Pacific, Indian, Arctic. I think that's all of the oceans there are."

My father went up to his bedroom, to talk to my mum and to be on the phone up there. I dropped the silver sixpence into my piggy bank. It was the kind of china piggy bank from which nothing could be removed. One day, when it could hold no more coins, I would be allowed to break it, but it was far from full.

III.

I never saw the white Mini again. Two days later, on Monday, my father took delivery of a black Rover, with cracked red leather seats. It was a bigger car than the Mini had been, but not as comfortable. The smell of old cigars permeated the leather upholstery, and long drives in the back of the Rover always left us feeling car-sick.

The black Rover was not the only thing to arrive on Monday morning. I also received a letter.

I was seven years old, and I never got letters. I got cards, on my birthday, from my grandparents, and from Ellen Henderson, my mother's friend whom I did not know. On my birthday Ellen Henderson, who lived in a camper van, would send me a handkerchief. I did not get letters. Even so, I would check the post every day to see if there was anything for me.

And, that morning, there was.

I opened it, did not understand what I was looking at, and took it to my mother.

"You've won the Premium Bonds," she said.

"What does that mean?"

"When you were born—when all of her grandchildren were born—your grandma bought you a Premium Bond. And when the number gets chosen you can win thousands of pounds."

"Did I win thousands of pounds?"

"No." She looked at the slip of paper. "You've won twenty-five pounds."

I was sad not to have won thousands of pounds (I already knew what I would buy with it. I would buy a place to go and be alone, like a Batcave, with a hidden entrance), but I was delighted to be in possession of a fortune beyond my previous imaginings. Twenty-five pounds. I could buy four little blackjack or fruit salad sweets for a penny: they were a farthing each, although there were no more farthings. Twenty-five pounds, at 240 pennies to the pound and four sweets to the penny, was . . . more sweets than I could easily imagine.

"I'll put it in your post office account," said my mother, crushing my dreams.

I did not have any more sweets than I had had that morning. Even so, I was rich. Twenty-five pounds richer than I had been moments before. I had never won anything, ever.

I made her show me the piece of paper with my name on it again, before she put it into her handbag.

That was Monday morning. In the afternoon the ancient Mr. Wollery, who came in on Monday and Thursday afternoons to do some gardening (Mrs. Wollery, his equally ancient wife, who wore galoshes, huge semi-transparent overshoes, would come in on Wednesday afternoons and clean), was digging in the vegetable garden and dug up a bottle filled with pennies and halfpennies and threepenny bits and even farthings. None of the coins was dated later than 1937, and I spent the afternoon polishing them with brown sauce and vinegar, to make them shine.

My mother put the bottle of old coins on the mantelpiece of the dining room, and said that she expected that a coin collector might pay several pounds for them.

I went to bed that night happy and excited. I was rich. Buried treasure had been discovered. The world was a good place.

I don't remember how the dreams started. But that's the way of dreams, isn't it? I know that I was in school, and having a bad day, hiding from the kinds of kids who hit me and called me names, but they found me anyway, deep in the rhododendron thicket behind the school, and I knew it must be a dream (but in the dream I didn't know this, it was real and it was true) because my grandfather was with them, and his friends, old men with gray skin and hacking coughs. They held sharp pencils, the kind that drew blood when you were jabbed with them. I ran from them, but they were faster than I was, the old men and the big boys, and, in the boys' toilets, where I had hidden in a cubicle, they caught up with me. They held me down, forced my mouth wide open.

My grandfather (but it was not my grandfather: it was really a waxwork of my grandfather, intent on selling me to *anatomy*) held something sharp and glittering, and he began pushing it into my mouth with his stubby fingers. It was hard and sharp and familiar, and it made me gag and choke. My mouth filled with a metallic taste.

They were looking at me with mean, triumphant eyes, all the people in the boys' toilets, and I tried not to choke on the thing in my throat, determined not to give them that satisfaction.

I woke and I was choking.

I could not breathe. There was something in my throat, hard and sharp and stopping me from breathing or from crying out. I began to cough as I woke, tears streaming down my cheeks, nose running.

I pushed my fingers as deeply as I could into my mouth, desperate and panicked and determined. With the tip of my forefinger I felt the edge of something hard. I put the middle finger on the other side of it, choking myself, clamping the thing between them, and I pulled whatever it was out of my throat.

I gasped for breath, and then I half-vomited onto my bedsheets, threw up a clear drool flecked with blood, from where the thing had cut my throat as I had pulled it out.

I did not look at the thing. It was tight in my hand, slimy with my saliva and my phlegm. I did not want to look at it. I did not want it to exist, the bridge between my dream and the waking world.

I ran down the hallway to the bathroom, down at the far end of the house. I washed my mouth out, drank directly from the cold tap, spat red into the white sink. Only when I'd done that did I sit on the side of the white bathtub and open my hand. I was scared.

But what was in my hand—what had been in my throat—wasn't scary. It was only a coin: a silver shilling.

I went back to the bedroom. I dressed myself, cleaned the vomit from my sheets as best I could with a damp face-flannel. I hoped that the sheets would dry before I had to sleep in the bed that night. Then I went downstairs.

I wanted to tell someone about the shilling, but I did not know who to tell. I knew enough about adults to know that if I did tell them what had happened, I would not be believed. Adults rarely seemed to believe me when I told the truth anyway. Why would they believe me about something so unlikely?

My sister was playing in the back garden with some of her friends. She ran over to me angrily when she saw me. She said, "I hate you. I'm telling Mummy and Daddy when they come home."

"What?"

"You know," she said. "I know it was you."

"What was me?"

"Throwing coins at me. At all of us. From the bushes. That was just nasty."

"But I didn't."

"It hurt."

She went back to her friends, and they all glared at me. My throat felt painful and ragged.

I walked down the drive. I don't know where I was thinking of going—I just didn't want to be there any longer.

Lettie Hempstock was standing at the bottom of the drive, beneath the chestnut trees. She looked as if she had been waiting for a hundred years and could wait for another hundred. She wore a white dress, but the light coming through the chestnut's young spring leaves stained it green.

I said, "Hello."

She said, "You were having bad dreams, weren't you?"

I took the shilling out of my pocket and showed it to her. "I was choking on it," I told her. "When I woke up. But I don't know how it got into my mouth. If someone had put it into my mouth, I would have woken up. It was just *in* there, when I woke."

"Yes," she said.

"My sister says I threw coins at them from the bushes, but I didn't."

"No," she agreed. "You didn't."

I said, "Lettie? What's happening?"

"Oh," she said, as if it was obvious. "Someone's just trying to give people money, that's all. But it's doing it very badly, and it's stirring things up around here that should be asleep. And that's not good."

"Is it something to do with the man who died?"

"Something to do with him. Yes."

"Is he doing this?"

She shook her head. Then she said, "Have you had breakfast?"

I shook my head.

"Well then," she said. "Come on."

We walked down the lane together. There were a few houses

down the lane, here and there, back then, and she pointed to them as we went past. "In that house," said Lettie Hempstock, "a man dreamed of being sold and of being turned into money. Now he's started seeing things in mirrors."

"What kinds of things?"

"Himself. But with fingers poking out of his eye sockets. And things coming out of his mouth. Like crab claws."

I thought about people with crab legs coming out of their mouths, in mirrors. "Why did I find a shilling in my throat?"

"He wanted people to have money."

"The opal miner? Who died in the car?"

"Yes. Sort of. Not exactly. He started this all off, like someone lighting a fuse on a firework. His death lit the touchpaper. The thing that's exploding right now, that isn't him. That's somebody else. Something else."

She rubbed her freckled nose with a grubby hand.

"A lady's gone mad in that house," she told me, and it would not have occurred to me to doubt her. "She has money in the mattress. Now she won't get out of bed, in case someone takes it from her."

"How do you know?"

She shrugged. "Once you've been around for a bit, you get to know stuff."

I kicked a stone. "By 'a bit' do you mean 'a really long time'?"

She nodded.

"How old are you, really?" I asked.

"Eleven."

I thought for a bit. Then I asked, "How long have you been eleven for?"

She smiled at me.

We walked past Caraway Farm. The farmers, whom one day I

would come to know as Callie Anders's parents, were standing in their farmyard, shouting at each other. They stopped when they saw us.

When we rounded a bend in the lane, and were out of sight, Lettie said, "Those poor people."

"Why are they poor people?"

"Because they've been having money problems. And this morning he had a dream where she . . . she was doing bad things. To earn money. So he looked in her handbag and found lots of folded-up ten-shilling notes. She says she doesn't know where they came from, and he doesn't believe her. He doesn't know what to believe."

"All the fighting and the dreams. It's about money, isn't it?"

"I'm not sure," said Lettie, and she seemed so grown-up then that I was almost scared of her.

"Whatever's happening," she said, eventually, "it can all be sorted out." She saw the expression on my face then, worried. Scared even. And she said, "After pancakes."

Lettie cooked us pancakes on a big metal griddle, on the kitchen stove. They were paper-thin, and as each pancake was done Lettie would squeeze lemon onto it, and plop a blob of plum jam into the center, and roll it tightly, like a cigar. When there were enough we sat at the kitchen table and wolfed them down.

There was a hearth in that kitchen, and there were ashes still smoldering in the hearth, from the night before. That kitchen was a friendly place, I thought.

I said to Lettie, "I'm scared."

She smiled at me. "I'll make sure you're safe. I promise. *I'm* not scared."

I was still scared, but not as much. "It's just scary."

"I said I promise," said Lettie Hempstock. "I won't let you be hurt."

"Hurt?" said a high, cracked voice. "Who's hurt? What's been hurt? Why would anybody be hurt?"

It was Old Mrs. Hempstock, her apron held between her hands, and in the hollow of the apron so many daffodils that the light reflected up from them transformed her face to gold, and the kitchen seemed bathed in yellow light.

Lettie said, "Something's causing trouble. It's giving people money. In their dreams and in real life." She showed the old lady my shilling. "My friend found himself choking on this shilling when he woke up this morning."

Old Mrs. Hempstock put her apron on the kitchen table, rapidly moved the daffodils off the cloth and onto the wood. Then she took the shilling from Lettie. She squinted at it, sniffed it, rubbed at it, listened to it (or put it to her ear, at any rate), then touched it with the tip of her purple tongue.

"It's new," she said, at last. "It says 1912 on it, but it didn't exist yesterday."

Lettie said, "I knew there was something funny about it."

I looked up at Old Mrs. Hempstock. "How do you know?"

"Good question, luvvie. It's electron decay, mostly. You have to look at things closely to see the electrons. They're the little dinky ones that look like tiny smiles. The neutrons are the gray ones that look like frowns. The electrons were all a bit too smiley for 1912, so then I checked the sides of the letters and the old king's head, and everything was a tad too crisp and sharp. Even where they were worn, it was as if they'd been made to be worn."

"You must have very good eyesight," I told her. I was impressed. She gave me back the coin.

"Not as good as it once was, but then, when you get to be my age, your eyesight won't be as sharp as it once was, neither." And she let out a guffaw as if she had said something very funny.

"How old is that?"

Lettie looked at me, and I was worried that I'd said something rude. Sometimes adults didn't like to be asked their ages, and sometimes they did. In my experience, old people did. They were proud of their ages. Mrs. Wollery was seventy-seven, and Mr. Wollery was eighty-nine, and they liked telling us how old they were.

Old Mrs. Hempstock went over to a cupboard, and took out several colorful vases. "Old enough," she said. "I remember when the moon was made."

"Hasn't there always been a moon?"

"Bless you. Not in the slightest. I remember the day the moon came. We looked up in the sky—it was all dirty brown and sooty gray here then, not green and blue . . ." She half-filled each of the vases at the sink. Then she took a pair of blackened kitchen scissors, and snipped off the bottom half-inch of stem from each of the daffodils.

I said, "Are you sure it's not that man's ghost doing this? Are you sure we aren't being haunted?"

They both laughed then, the girl and the old woman, and I felt stupid. I said, "Sorry."

"Ghosts can't make things," said Lettie. "They aren't even good at moving things."

Old Mrs. Hempstock said, "Go and get your mother. She's doing laundry." Then, to me, "You shall help me with the daffs."

I helped her put the flowers into the vases, and she asked my opinion on where to put the vases in the kitchen. We placed the vases where I suggested, and I felt wonderfully important.

The daffodils sat like patches of sunlight, making that dark wooden kitchen even more cheerful. The floor was made of red and gray flagstones. The walls were whitewashed.

The old woman gave me a lump of honeycomb, from the Hempstocks' own beehive, on a chipped saucer, and poured a little cream over it from a jug. I ate it with a spoon, chewing the wax like gum, letting the honey flow into my mouth, sweet and sticky with an aftertaste of wildflowers.

I was scraping the last of the cream and honey from the saucer when Lettie and her mother came into the kitchen. Mrs. Hempstock still had big Wellington boots on, and she strode in as if she were in an enormous hurry. "Mother!" she said. "Giving the boy honey. You'll rot his teeth."

Old Mrs. Hempstock shrugged. "I'll have a word with the wigglers in his mouth," she said. "Get them to leave his teeth alone."

"You can't just boss bacteria around like that," said the younger Mrs. Hempstock. "They don't like it."

"Stuff and silliness," said the old lady. "You leave wigglers alone and they'll be carrying on like anything. Show them who's boss and they can't do enough for you. You've tasted my cheese." She turned to me. "I've won medals for my cheese. Medals. Back in the old king's day there were those who'd ride for a week to buy a round of my cheese. They said that the king himself had it with his bread and his boys, Prince Dickon and Prince Geoffrey and even little Prince John, they swore it was the finest cheese they had ever tasted—"

"Gran," said Lettie, and the old lady stopped, mid-flow.

Lettie's mother said, "You'll be needing a hazel wand. And," she added, somewhat doubtfully, "I suppose you could take the lad. It's his coin, and it'll be easier to carry if he's with you. Something she made."

"She?" said Lettie.

She was holding her horn-handled penknife, with the blade closed.

"Tastes like a she," said Lettie's mother. "I might be wrong, mind."

"Don't take the boy," said Old Mrs. Hempstock. "Asking for trouble, that is."

I was disappointed.

"We'll be fine," said Lettie. "I'll take care of him. Him and me. It'll be an adventure. And he'll be company. Please, Gran?"

I looked up at Old Mrs. Hempstock with hope on my face, and waited.

"Don't say I didn't warn you, if it all goes wobbly," said Old Mrs. Hempstock.

"Thank you, Gran. I won't. And I'll be careful."

Old Mrs. Hempstock sniffed. "Now, don't do anything stupid. Approach it with care. Bind it, close its ways, send it back to sleep."

"I know," said Lettie. "I know all that. Honestly. We'll be fine."

That's what she said. But we weren't.

IV.

Lettie led me to a hazel thicket beside the old road (the hazel catkins were hanging heavy in the spring) and she broke off a thin branch. Then, with her knife, as if she had done it ten thousand times before, she stripped the branch of bark, cut it again, so now it resembled a Y. She put the knife away (I did not see where it went) and held the two ends of the Y in her hands.

"I'm not dowsing," she told me. "Just using it as a guide. We're looking for a blue . . . a bluebottle, I think to start with. Or something purply-blue, and shiny."

I looked around with her. "I can't see one."

"It'll be here," she assured me.

I gazed around, taking in the grass, a reddish-brown chicken pecking at the side of the driveway, some rusty farm machinery, the wooden trestle table beside the road and the six empty metal milk churns that sat upon it. I saw the Hempstocks' red-brick farmhouse, crouched and comfortable like an animal at rest. I saw the spring flowers; the omnipresent white and yellow daisies, the golden dandelions and do-you-like-butter buttercups, and, late in the season, a lone bluebell in the shadows beneath the milk-churn table, still glistening with dew . . .

"That?" I asked.

"You've got sharp eyes," she said, approvingly.

We walked together to the bluebell. Lettie closed her eyes when
we reached it. She moved her body back and forth, the hazel wand
extended, as if she were the central point on a clock or a compass, her
wand the hands, orienting toward a midnight or an east that I could
not perceive. "Black," she said suddenly, as if she were describing
something from a dream. "And soft."

We walked away from the bluebell, along the lane that I imagined, sometimes, must have been a Roman road. We were a hundred
yards up the lane, near where the Mini had been parked, when she
spotted it: a scrap of black cloth caught on the barbed wire of the
fence.

Lettie approached it. Again, the outstretched hazel stick, again
the slow turning and turning. "Red," she said, with certainty. "Very
red. That way."

We walked together in the direction she indicated. Across a
meadow and into a clump of trees. "There," I said, fascinated. The
corpse of a very small animal—a vole, by the look of it—lay on a
clump of green moss. It had no head, and bright blood stained its fur
and beaded on the moss. It was very red.

"Now, from here on," said Lettie, "hold on to my arm. Don't let go."

I put out my right hand and took her left arm, just below the
elbow. She moved the hazel wand. "This way," she said.

"What are we looking for now?"

"We're getting closer," she said. "The next thing we're looking
for is a storm."

We pushed our way into a clump of trees, and through the
clump of trees into a wood, and squeezed our way through trees
too close together, their foliage a thick canopy above our heads. We
found a clearing in the wood, and walked along the clearing, in a
world made green.

From our left came a mumble of distant thunder.

"Storm," sang Lettie. She let her body swing again, and I turned with her, holding her arm. I felt, or imagined I felt, a throbbing going through me, holding her arm, as if I were touching mighty engines.

She set off in a new direction. We crossed a tiny stream together. Then she stopped, suddenly, and stumbled, but did not fall.

"Are we there?" I asked.

"Not there," she said. "No. It knows we're coming. It feels us. And it does not want us to come to it."

The hazel wand was whipping around now like a magnet being pushed at a repelling pole. Lettie grinned.

A gust of wind threw leaves and dirt up into our faces. In the distance I could hear something rumble, like a train. It was getting harder to see, and the sky that I could make out above the canopy of leaves was dark, as if huge storm-clouds had moved above our heads, or as if it had gone from morning directly to twilight.

Lettie shouted, "Get down!" and she crouched on the moss, pulling me down with her. She lay prone, and I lay beside her, feeling a little silly. The ground was damp.

"How long will we——?"

"Shush!" She sounded almost angry. I said nothing.

Something came through the woods, above our heads. I glanced up, saw something brown and furry, but flat, like a huge rug, flapping and curling at the edges, and, at the front of the rug, a mouth, filled with dozens of tiny sharp teeth, facing down.

It flapped and floated above us, and then it was gone.

"What was that?" I asked, my heart pounding so hard in my chest that I did not know if I would be able to stand again.

"Manta wolf," said Lettie. "We've already gone a bit further out than I thought." She got to her feet and stared the way the furry thing had gone. She raised the tip of the hazel wand, and turned around slowly.

"I'm not getting anything." She tossed her head, to get the hair out of her eyes, without letting go of the fork of hazel wand. "Either it's hiding or we're too close." She bit her lip. Then she said, "The shilling. The one from your throat. Bring it out."

I took it from my pocket with my left hand, offered it to her.

"No," she said. "I can't touch it, not right now. Put it down on the fork of the stick."

I didn't ask why. I just put the silver shilling down at the intersection of the Y. Lettie stretched her arms out, and turned very slowly, with the end of the stick pointing straight out. I moved with her, but felt nothing. No throbbing engines. We were over halfway around when she stopped and said, "Look!"

I looked in the direction she was facing, but I saw nothing but trees, and shadows in the wood.

"No, look. There." She indicated with her head.

The tip of the hazel wand had begun smoking, softly. She turned a little to the left, a little to the right, a little further to the right again, and the tip of the wand began to glow a bright orange.

"That's something I've not seen before," said Lettie. "I'm using the coin as an amplifier, but it's as if—"

There was a *whoompf!* and the end of the stick burst into flame. Lettie pushed it down into the damp moss. She said, "Take your coin back," and I did, picking it up carefully, in case it was hot, but it was icy cold. She left the hazel wand behind on the moss, the charcoal tip of it still smoking irritably.

Lettie walked and I walked beside her. We held hands now, my right hand in her left. The air smelled strange, like fireworks, and the world grew darker with every step we took into the forest.

"I said I'd keep you safe, didn't I?" said Lettie.

"Yes."

"I promised I wouldn't let anything hurt you."

"Yes."

She said, "Just keep holding my hand. Don't let go. Whatever happens, don't let go."

Her hand was warm, but not sweaty. It was reassuring.

"Hold my hand," she repeated. "And don't do anything unless I tell you. You've got that?"

I said, "I don't feel very safe."

She did not argue. She said, "We've gone further than I imagined. Further than I expected. I'm not really sure what kinds of things live out here on the margins."

The trees ended, and we walked out into open country.

I said, "Are we a long way from your farm?"

"No. We're still on the borders of the farm. Hempstock Farm stretches a very long way. We brought a lot of this with us from the old country, when we came here. The farm came with us, and brought things with it when it came. Gran calls them fleas."

I did not know where we were, but I could not believe we were still on the Hempstocks' land, no more than I believed we were in the world I had grown up in. The sky of this place was the dull orange of a warning light; the plants, which were spiky, like huge, ragged aloes, were a dark silvery green, and looked as if they had been beaten from gunmetal.

The coin, in my left hand, which had warmed to the heat of my body, began to cool down again, until it was as cold as an ice cube. My right hand held Lettie Hempstock's hand as tightly as I could.

She said, "We're here."

I thought I was looking at a building at first: that it was some kind of tent, as high as a country church, made of gray and pink canvas that flapped in the gusts of storm wind, in that orange sky: a lopsided canvas structure aged by weather and ripped by time.

And then it turned and I saw its face, and I heard something make a whimpering sound, like a dog that had been kicked, and I realized that the thing that was whimpering was me.

Its face was ragged, and its eyes were deep holes in the fabric. There was nothing behind it, just a gray canvas mask, huger than I could have imagined, all ripped and torn, blowing in the gusts of storm wind.

Something shifted, and the ragged thing looked down at us.

Lettie Hempstock said, "Name yourself."

There was a pause. Empty eyes stared down at us. Then a voice as featureless as the wind said, "I am the lady of this place. I have been here for such a long time. Since before the little people sacrificed each other on the rocks. My name is my own, child. Not yours. Now leave me be, before I blow you all away." It gestured with a limb like a broken mainsail, and I felt myself shivering.

Lettie Hempstock squeezed my hand and I felt braver. She said, "Asked you to name yourself, I did. I en't heard more'n empty boasts of age and time. Now, you tell me your name and I en't asking you a third time." She sounded more like a country girl than she ever had before. Perhaps it was the anger in her voice: her words came out differently when she was angry.

"No," whispered the gray thing, flatly. "Little girl, little girl . . . who's your friend?"

Lettie whispered, "Don't say nothing." I nodded, pressed my lips tightly together.

"I am growing tired of this," said the gray thing, with a petulant shake of its ragged cloth arms. "Something came to me, and pleaded for love and help. It told me how I could make all the things like it happy. That they are simple creatures, and all any of them want is money, just money, and nothing more. Little tokens-of-work. If it had asked, I would have given them wisdom, or peace, perfect peace . . ."

"None of that," said Lettie Hempstock. "You've got nothing to give them that they want. Let them be."

The wind gusted and the gargantuan figure flapped with it, huge sails swinging, and when the wind was done the creature had changed position. Now it seemed to have crouched lower to the ground, and it was examining us like an enormous canvas scientist looking at two white mice.

Two very scared white mice, holding hands.

Lettie's hand was sweating, now. She squeezed my hand, whether to reassure me or herself I did not know, and I squeezed her hand back.

The ripped face, the place where the face should have been, twisted. I thought it was smiling. Perhaps it was smiling. I felt as if it was examining me, taking me apart. As if it knew everything about me—things I did not even know about myself.

The girl holding my hand said, "If you en't telling me your name, I'll bind you as a nameless thing. And you'll still be bounden, tied and sealed like a polter or a shuck."

She waited, but the thing said nothing, and Lettie Hempstock began to say words in a language I did not know. Sometimes she was talking, and sometimes it was more like singing, in a tongue that was nothing I had ever heard, or would ever encounter later in life. I knew the tune, though. It was a child's song, the tune to which we sang the nursery rhyme "Girls and Boys Come Out to Play." That was the tune, but her words were older words. I was certain of that.

And as she sang, things happened, beneath the orange sky.

The earth writhed and churned with worms, long gray worms that pushed up from the ground beneath our feet.

Something came hurtling at us from the center mass of flapping canvas. It was a little bigger than a football. At school, during games, mostly I dropped things I was meant to catch, or closed my hand on them a moment too late, letting them hit me in the face or the stomach. But this thing was coming straight at me and Lettie Hempstock, and I did not think, I only *did*.

I put both my hands out and I caught the thing, a flapping, writhing mass of cobwebs and rotting cloth. And as I caught it in my hands I felt something hurt me: a stabbing pain in the sole of my foot, momentary and then gone, as if I had trodden upon a pin.

Lettie knocked the thing I was holding out of my hands, and it fell to the ground, where it collapsed into itself. She grabbed my right hand, held it firmly once more. And through all this, she continued to sing.

I have dreamed of that song, of the strange words to that simple rhyme-song, and on several occasions I have understood what she was saying, in my dreams. In those dreams I spoke that language too, the first language, and I had dominion over the nature of all that was real. In my dream, it was the tongue of what is, and anything spoken in it becomes real, because nothing said in that language can be a lie. It is the most basic building brick of everything. In my dreams I have used that language to heal the sick and to fly; once I dreamed I kept a perfect little bed-and-breakfast by the seaside, and to everyone who came to stay with me I would say, in that tongue, "Be whole," and they would become whole, not be broken people, not any longer, because I had spoken the language of shaping.

And, because Lettie was speaking the language of shaping, even if I did not understand what she was saying, I understood what was being said. The thing in the clearing was being bound to that place for always, trapped, forbidden to exercise its influence on anything beyond its own domain.

Lettie Hempstock finished her song.

In my mind, I thought I could hear the creature screaming, protesting, railing, but the place beneath that orange sky was quiet. Only the flapping of canvas and the rattle of twigs in the wind broke the silence.

The wind died down.

A thousand pieces of torn gray cloth settled on the black earth like dead things, or like so much abandoned laundry. Nothing moved.

Lettie said, "That should hold it." She squeezed my hand. I thought she was trying to sound bright, but she didn't. She sounded grim. "Let's take you home."

We walked, hand in hand, through a wood of blue-tinged ever-greens, and we crossed a lacquered red and yellow bridge over an ornamental pond; we walked along the edge of a field in which young corn was coming up, like green grass planted in rows; we climbed a wooden stile, hand in hand, and reached another field, planted with what looked like small reeds or furry snakes, black and white and brown and orange and gray and striped, all of them waving gently, curling and uncurling in the sun.

"What are they?" I asked.

"You can pull one up and see, if you like," said Lettie.

I looked down: the furry tendril by my feet was perfectly black. I bent, grasped it at the base, firmly, with my left hand, and I pulled.

Something came up from the earth, and swung around angrily. My hand felt like a dozen tiny needles had been sunk into it. I brushed the earth from it, and apologized, and it stared at me, more with surprise and puzzlement than with anger. It jumped from my hand to my shirt, I stroked it: a kitten, black and sleek, with a pointed, inquisitive face, a white spot over one ear, and eyes of a peculiarly vivid blue-green.

"At the farm, we get our cats the normal way," said Lettie.

"What's that?"

"Big Oliver. He turned up at the farm back in pagan times. All our farm cats trace back to him."

I looked at the kitten hanging on my shirt with tiny kitten-claws.

"Can I take it home?" I asked.

"It's not an it. It's a *she*. Not a good idea, taking anything home from these parts," said Lettie.

I put the kitten down at the edge of the field. She darted off after a butterfly, which floated up and out of her reach, then she scampered away, without a look back.

"My kitten was run over," I told Lettie. "It was only little. The man who died told me about it, although he wasn't driving. He said they didn't see it."

"I'm sorry," said Lettie. We were walking beneath a canopy of apple-blossom then, and the world smelled like honey. "That's the trouble with living things. Don't last very long. Kittens one day, old cats the next. And then just memories. And the memories fade and blend and smudge together . . ."

She opened a five-bar gate, and we went through it. She let go of my hand. We were at the bottom of the lane, near the wooden shelf by the road with the battered silver milk churns on it. The world smelled normal.

I said, "We're really back, now?"

"Yes," said Lettie Hempstock. "And we won't be seeing any more trouble from her." She paused. "Big, wasn't she? And nasty? I've not seen one like that before. If I'd known she was going to be so old, and so big, and so nasty, I wouldn't've brung you with me."

I was glad that she had taken me with her.

Then she said, "I wish you hadn't let go of my hand. But still, you're all right, aren't you? Nothing went wrong. No damage done."

I said, "I'm fine. Not to worry. I'm a brave soldier." That was what my grandfather always said. Then I repeated what she had said, "No damage done."

She smiled at me, a bright, relieved smile, and I hoped I had said the right thing.

V.

That evening my sister sat on her bed, brushing her hair over and over. She brushed it a hundred times every night, and counted each brush stroke. I did not know why.

"What are you doing?" she asked.

"Looking at my foot," I told her.

I was staring at the sole of my right foot. There was a pink line across the center of the sole, from the ball of the foot almost to the heel, where I had stepped on a broken glass as a toddler. I remember waking up in my cot, the morning after it happened, looking at the black stitches that held the edges of the cut together. It was my earliest memory. I was used to the pink scar. The little hole beside it, in the arch of my foot, was new. It was where the sudden sharp pain had been, although it did not hurt. It was just a hole.

I prodded it with my forefinger, and it seemed to me that something inside the hole retreated.

My sister had stopped brushing her hair and was watching me curiously. I got up, walked out of the bedroom, down the corridor, to the bathroom at the end of the hall.

I do not know why I did not ask an adult about it. I do not remember asking adults about anything, except as a last resort. That was the year I dug out a wart from my knee with a penknife, discovering how deeply I could cut before it hurt, and what the roots of a wart looked like.

In the bathroom cupboard, behind the mirror, was a pair of stainless steel tweezers, the kind with pointed sharp tips, for pulling out wooden splinters, and a box of sticking plasters. I sat on the metal side of the white bathtub and examined the hole in my foot. It was a simple, small round hole, smooth-edged. I could not see how deeply it went, because something was in the way. Something was blocking it. Something that seemed to retreat, as the light touched it.

I held my tweezers, and I watched. Nothing happened. Nothing changed.

I put the forefinger of my left hand over the hole, gently, blocking the light. Then I put the tip of the tweezers beside the hole and I waited. I counted to a hundred—inspired, perhaps, by my sister's hair-brushing. Then I pulled my finger away and stabbed in with the tweezers.

I caught the head of the worm, if that was what it was, by the tip, between the metal prongs, and I squeezed it, and I pulled.

Have you ever tried to pull a worm from a hole? You know how hard they can hold on? The way they use their whole bodies to grip the sides of the hole? I pulled perhaps an inch of this worm—pink and gray, streaked, like something infected—out of the hole in my foot, and then felt it stop. I could feel it, inside my flesh, making itself rigid, unpullable. I was not scared by this. It was obviously just something that happened to people, like when the neighbor's cat, Misty, had worms. I had a worm in my foot, and I was removing the worm.

I twisted the tweezers, thinking, I suspect, of spaghetti on a fork, winding the worm around the tweezers. It tried to pull back, but I turned it, a little at a time, until I could definitely pull no further.

I could feel, inside me, the sticky plastic way that it tried to hold on, like a strip of pure muscle. I leaned over, as far as I could, reached out my left hand and turned on the bath's hot-water tap, the one with the red dot in the center, and I let it run. The water ran for three, four minutes out of the tap and down the plug hole before it began to steam.

When the water was steaming, I extended my foot and my right arm, maintaining pressure on the tweezers and on the inch of the creature that I had wound out of my body. Then I put the place where the tweezers were under the hot tap. The water splashed my foot, but my soles were barefoot-hardened, and I scarcely minded. The water that touched my fingers scalded them, but I was prepared for the heat. The worm wasn't. I felt it flex inside me, trying to pull back from the scalding water, felt it loosen its grip on the inside of my foot. I turned the tweezers, triumphantly, like picking the best scab in the world, as the creature began to come out of me, putting up less and less resistance.

I pulled at it, steadily, and as it went under the hot water it slackened, until the end. It was almost all out of me—I could feel it—but I was too confident, too triumphant, and impatient, and I tugged too quickly, too hard, and the worm came off in my hand. The end of it that came out of me was oozing and broken, as if it had snapped off.

Still, if the creature had left anything behind in my foot, it was tiny.

I examined the worm. It was dark gray and light gray, streaked with pink, and segmented, like a normal earthworm. Now it was out of the hot water, it seemed to be recovering. It wriggled, and the body that had been wrapped around the tweezers now dangled, writhing, although it hung from the head (*Was* it its head? How could I tell?) where I had pinched it.

I did not want to kill it—I did not kill animals, not if I could help it—but I had to get rid of it. It was dangerous. I had no doubt of that.

I held the worm above the bath's plug hole, where it wriggled, under the scalding water. Then I let it go, and watched it vanish down the drain. I let the water run for a while, and I washed off the tweezers. Finally I put a small sticking plaster over the hole in the sole of my foot, and put the plug in the bath, to prevent the worm from climbing back up the open plug hole, before I turned off the tap. I did not know if it was dead, but I did not think you came back from the drain.

I put the tweezers back where I had got them from, behind the bathroom mirror, then I closed the mirror and stared at myself.

I wondered, as I wondered so often when I was that age, who *I* was, and what exactly was looking at the face in the mirror. If the face I was looking at wasn't me, and I knew it wasn't, because I would still be me whatever happened to my face, then what *was* me? And what was watching?

I went back to the bedroom. It was my night to have the door to the hallway open, and I waited until my sister was asleep, and wouldn't tell on me, and then, in the dim light from the hall, I read a *Secret Seven* mystery until I fell asleep.

VI.

An admission about myself: as a very small boy, perhaps three or four years old, I could be a monster. "You were a little *momzer*," several aunts told me, on different occasions, once I had safely reached adulthood and my dreadful infant deeds could be recalled with wry amusement. But I do not actually remember being a monster. I just remember wanting my own way.

Small children believe themselves to be gods, or some of them do, and they can only be satisfied when the rest of the world goes along with their way of seeing things.

But I was no longer a small boy. I was seven. I had been fearless, but now I was such a frightened child.

The incident of the worm in my foot did not scare me. I did not talk about it. I wondered, though, the next day, whether people often got foot-worms, or whether it was something that had only ever happened to me, in the orange-sky place on the edge of the Hempstocks' farm.

I peeled off the plaster on the sole of my foot when I awoke, and was relieved to see that the hole had begun to close up. There was a pink place where it had been, like a blood blister, but nothing more.

I went down to breakfast. My mother looked happy. She said, "Good news, darling. I've got a job. They need an optometrist at Dicksons Opticians, and they want me to start this afternoon. I'll be working four days a week."

I did not mind. I would be fine on my own.

"And I've got more good news. We have someone coming to look after you children while I'm away. Her name is Ursula. She'll be sleeping in your old bedroom, at the top of the stairs. She'll be a sort of housekeeper. She'll make sure you children are fed, and she'll clean the house—Mrs. Wollery is having trouble with her hip, and she says it will be a few weeks before she can come back. It will be such a load off my mind to have someone here, if Daddy and I are both working."

"You don't have the money," I said. "You said you didn't have any money."

"That's why I'm taking the optometrist job," she said. "And Ursula's looking after you for room and board. She needs to live locally for a few months. She phoned this morning. Her references are excellent."

I hoped that she would be nice. The previous housekeeper, Gertruda, six months earlier, had not been nice: she had enjoyed playing practical jokes on my sister and me. She would short-sheet the beds, for example, which left us baffled. Eventually we had marched outside the house with placards saying "We hate Gertruda" and "We do not like Gertruda's cooking," and put tiny frogs in her bed, and she had gone back to Sweden.

I took a book and went out into the garden.

It was a warm spring day, and sunny, and I climbed up a rope ladder to the lowest branch of the big beech tree, sat on it, and read my book. I was not scared of anything, when I read my book: I was far away, in ancient Egypt, learning about Hathor, and how she had stalked Egypt in the form of a lioness, and she had killed so many people that the sands of Egypt turned red, and how they had only defeated her by mixing beer and honey and sleeping draughts, and dying this concoction red, so she thought it was blood, and she drank it, and fell asleep. Ra, the father of the gods, made her the goddess of love after that, so the wounds she had inflicted on people would now only be wounds of the heart.

I wondered why the gods had done that. Why hadn't they just killed her, when they had the chance?

I liked myths. They weren't adult stories and they weren't children's stories. They were better than that. They just *were*.

Adult stories never made sense, and they were so slow to start. They made me feel like there were secrets, Masonic, mythic secrets, to adulthood. Why didn't adults want to read about Narnia, about secret islands and smugglers and dangerous fairies?

I was getting hungry. I climbed down from my tree, and went to the back of the house, past the laundry room that smelled of laundry soap and mildew, past the little coal-and-wood shed, past the outside toilet where the spiders hung and waited, wooden doors painted garden green. In through the back door, along the hallway and into the kitchen.

My mother was in there with a woman I had never seen before. When I saw her, my heart hurt. I mean that literally, not metaphorically: there was a momentary twinge in my chest—just a flash, and then it was gone.

My sister was sitting at the kitchen table, eating a bowl of cereal.

The woman was very pretty. She had shortish honey-blonde hair, huge gray-blue eyes, and pale lipstick. She seemed tall, even for an adult.

"Darling? This is Ursula Monkton," said my mother. I said nothing. I just stared at her. My mother nudged me.

"Hello," I said.

"He's shy," said Ursula Monkton. "I am certain that once he

warms up to me we shall be great friends." She reached out a hand and patted my sister's mousey-brown hair. My sister smiled a gap-toothed smile.

"I like you *so* much," my sister said. Then she said, to our mother and me, "When I grow up I want to be Ursula Monkton."

My mother and Ursula laughed. "You little dear," said Ursula Monkton. Then she turned to me. "And what about us, eh? Are we friends as well?"

I just looked at her, all grown-up and blonde, in her gray and pink skirt, and I was scared.

Her dress wasn't ragged. It was just the fashion of the thing, I suppose, the kind of dress that it was. But when I looked at her I imagined her dress flapping, in that windless kitchen, flapping like the mainsail of a ship, on a lonely ocean, under an orange sky.

I don't know what I said in reply, or if I even said anything. But I went out of that kitchen, although I was hungry, without even an apple.

I took my book into the back garden, beneath the balcony, by the flower bed that grew beneath the television room window, and I read—forgetting my hunger in Egypt with animal-headed gods who cut each other up and then restored one another to life again.

My sister came out into the garden.

"I like her so much," she told me. "She's my friend. Do you want to see what she gave me?" She produced a small gray purse, the kind my mother kept in her handbag for her coins, that fastened with a metal butterfly clip. It looked like it was made of leather. I wondered if it was mouse skin. She opened the purse, put her fingers into the opening, came out with a large silver coin: half a crown.

"Look!" she said. "Look what I got!"

I wanted a half a crown. No, I wanted what I could buy with half a crown—magic tricks and plastic joke-toys, and books, and, oh, so many things. But I did not want a little gray purse with a half a crown in it.

"I don't like her," I told my sister.

"That's only because I saw her first," said my sister. "She's *my* friend."

I did not think that Ursula Monkton was anybody's friend. I wanted to go and warn Lettie Hempstock about her—but what could I say? That the new housekeeper-nanny wore gray and pink? That she looked at me oddly?

I wished I had never let go of Lettie's hand. Ursula Monkton was my fault, I was certain of it, and I would not be able to get rid of her by flushing her down a plug hole, or putting frogs in her bed.

I should have left then, should have run away, fled down the lane the mile or so to the Hempstocks' farm, but I didn't, and then a taxi took my mother away to Dicksons Opticians, where she would show people letters through lenses, and help them see more clearly, and I was left there with Ursula Monkton.

She came out into the garden with a plate of sandwiches.

"I've spoken to your mother," she said, a sweet smile beneath the pale lipstick, "and while I'm here, you children need to limit your travels. You can be anywhere in the house or in the garden, or I will walk with you to your friends', but you may not leave the property and simply go wandering."

"Of course," said my sister.

I did not say anything.

My sister ate a peanut butter sandwich.

I was starving. I wondered whether the sandwiches were dangerous or not. I did not know. I was scared that I would eat one and it would turn into worms in my stomach, and that they would wriggle through me, colonizing my body, until they pushed out of my skin.

I went back into the house. I pushed the kitchen door open.

Ursula Monkton was not there. I stuffed my pockets with fruit, with apples and oranges and hard brown pears. I took three bananas and stuffed them down my jumper, and fled to my laboratory.

My laboratory—that was what I called it—was a green-painted shed as far away from the house as you could get, built up against the side of the house's huge old garage. A fig tree grew beside the shed, although we had never tasted ripe fruit from the tree, only seen the huge leaves and the green fruits. I called the shed my laboratory be-cause I kept my chemistry set in there: the chemistry set, a perennial birthday present, had been banished from the house by my father, after I had made something in a test tube. I had randomly mixed things together, and then heated them, until they had erupted and turned black, with an ammoniac stench that refused to fade. My father had said that he did not mind my doing experiments (although neither of us knew what I could possibly have been experimenting on, but that did not matter; my mother had been given chemistry sets for her birthday, and see how well that had turned out?) but he did not want them within smelling range of the house.

I ate a banana and a pear, then hid the rest of the fruit beneath the wooden table.

Adults follow paths. Children explore. Adults are content to walk the same way, hundreds of times, or thousands; perhaps it never occurs to adults to step off the paths, to creep beneath rhododendrons, to find the spaces between fences. I was a child, which meant that I knew a dozen different ways of getting out of our property and into the lane, ways that would not involve walking down our drive. I decided that I would creep out of the laboratory shed, along the wall to the edge of the lawn and then into the azaleas and bay laurels that bordered the garden there. From the laurels, I would slip down the hill and over the rusting metal fence that ran along the side of the lane.

Nobody was looking. I ran and I crept and got through the laurels, and I went down the hill, pushing through the brambles and the nettle patches that had sprung up since the last time I went that way.

Ursula Monkton was waiting for me at the bottom of the hill, just in front of the rusting metal fence. There was no way she could have got there without my seeing her, but she was there. She folded her arms and looked at me, and her gray and pink dress flapped in a gust of wind.

"I believe I said that you were not to leave the property."

"I'm not," I told her, with a cockiness I knew I did not feel, not even a little. "I'm still on the property. I'm just exploring."

"You're sneaking around," she said.

I said nothing.

"I think you should be in your bedroom, where I can keep an eye on you. It's time for your nap."

I was too old for naps, but I knew that I was too young to argue, or to win the argument if I did.

"Okay," I said.

"Don't say 'okay,'" she said. "Say 'Yes, Miss Monkton.' Or 'Ma'am.' Say 'Yes, ma'am.'" She looked down at me with her blue-gray eyes, which put me in mind of holes rotted in canvas, and which did not look pretty at that moment.

I said, "Yes, ma'am," and hated myself for saying it.

We walked together up the hill.

"Your parents can no longer afford this place," said Ursula Monkton. "And they can't afford to keep it up. Soon enough they'll see that the way to solve their financial problems is to sell this house and its gardens to property developers. Then all of *this*"—and *this* was the tangle of brambles, the unkempt world behind the lawn— "will become a dozen identical houses and gardens. And if you are lucky, you'll get to live in one. And if not, you will just envy the people who do. Will you like that?"

I loved the house, and the garden. I loved the rambling shabbiness of it. I loved that place as if it was a part of me, and perhaps, in some ways, it was.

"Who are you?" I asked.

"Ursula Monkton. I'm your housekeeper."

I said, "Who are you really? Why are you giving people money?"

"Everybody wants money," she said, as if it were self-evident. "It makes them happy. It will make you happy, if you let it." We had come out by the heap of grass clippings, behind the circle of green grass that we called the fairy ring: sometimes, when the weather was wet, it filled with vivid yellow toadstools.

"Now," she said. "Go to your room."

I ran from her—ran as fast as I could, across the fairy ring, up the lawn, past the rosebushes, past the coal shed and into the house.

Ursula Monkton was standing just inside the back door of the house to welcome me in, although she could not have got past me. I would have seen. Her hair was perfect, and her lipstick seemed freshly applied.

"I've been inside you," she said. "So a word to the wise. If you tell anybody anything, they won't believe you. And, because I've been inside you, I'll know. And I can make it so you never say anything I don't want you to say to anybody, not ever again."

I went upstairs to the bedroom, and I lay on my bed. The place on the sole of my foot where the worm had been throbbed and ached, and now my chest hurt too. I went away in my head, into a book. That was where I went whenever real life was too hard or too inflexible. I pulled down a handful of my mother's old books, from when she was a girl, and I read about schoolgirls having adventures in the 1930s and 1940s. Mostly they were up against smugglers or spies or fifth columnists, whatever they were, and the girls were always brave and they always knew exactly what to do. I was not brave and I had no idea what to do.

I had never felt so alone.

I wondered if the Hempstocks had a telephone. It seemed unlikely, but not impossible—perhaps it had been Mrs. Hempstock who had reported the abandoned Mini to the police in the first place. The phone book was downstairs, but I knew the number to call Directory Enquiries, and I only had to ask for anybody named Hempstock living at Hempstock Farm. There was a phone in my parents' bedroom.

I got off the bed, went to the doorway, looked out. The upstairs hallway was empty. As quickly, as quietly as I could, I walked into the bedroom next to mine. The walls were pale pink, my parents' bed covered with a bedspread covered in its turn with huge printed roses. There were French windows to the balcony that ran along that side of the house. There was a cream-colored telephone on the cream-and-gilt nightstand beside the bed. I picked it up, heard the dull whirring noise of the dial tone, and dialed Directory Enquiries, my finger pulling the holes in the dial down, a one, a nine, a two, and I waited for the operator to come on the line, and tell me the number of the Hempstocks' farm. I had a pencil with me, and I was ready to write the telephone number down in the back of a blue cloth-bound book called *Pansy Saves the School*.

The operator did not come on. The dialing tone continued, and over it, I heard Ursula Monkton's voice saying, "Properly brought-up young people would not even think about sneaking off to use the telephone, would they?"

I did not say anything, although I have no doubt she could hear me breathing. I put the handset down on the cradle, and went back into the bedroom I shared with my sister.

I sat on my bed, and stared out of the window.

My bed was pushed up hard against the wall just below the window. I loved to sleep with the windows open. Rainy nights were the best of all: I would open my windows and put my head on my pillow and close my eyes and feel the wind on my face and listen to the trees sway and creak. There would be raindrops blown onto my face, too, if I was lucky, and I would imagine that I was in my boat on the ocean and that it was swaying with the swell of the sea. I did not imagine that I was a pirate, or that I was going anywhere. I was just on my boat.

But now it was not raining, and it was not night. All I could see through the window were trees, and clouds, and the distant purple of horizon.

I had emergency chocolate supplies hidden beneath the large plastic Batman figurine I had acquired on my birthday, and I ate them, and as I ate them I thought of how I had let go of Lettie Hempstock's hand to grab the ball of rotting cloth, and I remembered the stabbing pain in my foot that had followed.

I brought her here, I thought, and I knew that it was true.

Ursula Monkton wasn't real. She was a cardboard mask for the thing that had traveled inside me as a worm, that had flapped and gusted in the open country under that orange sky.

I went back to reading *Pansy Saves the School.* The secret plans to the airbase next door to the school were being smuggled out to the enemy by spies who were teachers working on the school vegetable allotment: the plans were concealed inside hollowed-out vegetable marrows.

> *"Great heavens!" said Inspector Davidson of Scotland Yard's renowned Smugglers and Secret Spies Division (the SSSD). "That is literally the last place we would have looked!"*

"We owe you an apology, Pansy," said the stern headmistress, with an uncharacteristically warm smile, and a twinkle in her eyes that made Pansy think perhaps she had misjudged the woman all this term. "You have saved the reputation of the school! Now, before you get too full of yourself—aren't there some French verbs you ought to be conjugating for Madame?"

I could be happy with Pansy, in some part of my head, even while the rest of my head was filled with fear. I waited for my parents to come home. I would tell them what was happening. I would tell them. They would believe me.

At that time my father worked in an office an hour's drive away. I was not certain what he did. He had a very nice, pretty secretary, with a toy poodle, and whenever she knew we children would be coming in to see our father she would bring the poodle in from home, and we would play with it. Sometimes we would pass buildings and my father would say, "That's one of ours." But I did not care about buildings, so never asked how it was one of ours, or even who *we* were.

I lay on my bed, reading book after book, until Ursula Monkton appeared in the doorway of the room and said, "You can come down now."

My sister was watching television downstairs, in the television room. She was watching a program called *How*, a pop-science-and-how-things-work show, which opened with the hosts in Native American headdresses saying, "How?" and doing embarrassing war whoops.

I wanted to turn over to the BBC, but my sister looked at me triumphantly and said, "Ursula says it can stay on whatever I want to watch and you aren't allowed to change it."

I sat with her for a minute, as an old man with a moustache showed all the children of England how to tie fishing flies.

I said, "She's not nice."

"I like her. She's pretty."

My mother arrived home five minutes later, called hello from the corridor, then went into the kitchen to see Ursula Monkton. She reappeared. "Dinner will be ready as soon as Daddy gets home. Wash your hands."

My sister went upstairs and washed her hands.

I said to my mother, "I don't like her. Will you make her go away?"

My mother sighed. "It is *not* going to be Gertruda all over again, dear. Ursula's a very nice girl, from a very good family. And she positively *adores* the two of you."

My father came home, and dinner was served. A thick vegetable soup, then roast chicken and new potatoes with frozen peas. I loved all of the things on the table. I did not eat any of it.

"I'm not hungry," I explained.

"I'm not one for telling tales out of school," said Ursula Monkton, "but someone had chocolate on his hands and face when he came down from his bedroom."

"I wish you wouldn't eat that rubbish," grumbled my father.

"It's just processed sugar. And it ruins your appetite and your teeth," said my mother.

I was scared they would force me to eat, but they didn't. I sat there hungrily, while Ursula Monkton laughed at all my father's jokes. It seemed to me that he was making special jokes, just for her.

After dinner we all watched *Mission: Impossible*. I usually liked *Mission: Impossible*, but this time it made me feel uneasy, as people kept pulling their faces off to reveal new faces beneath. They were wearing rubber masks, and it was always our heroes underneath, but I wondered what would happen if Ursula Monkton pulled off her face, what would be underneath that?

We went to bed. It was my sister's night, and the bedroom door was closed. I missed the light in the hall. I lay in bed with the window open, wide awake, listening to the noises an old house makes at the end of a long day, and I wished as hard as I could, hoping my wishes could become real. I wished that my parents would send Ursula Monkton away, and then I would go down to the Hempstocks' farm, and tell Lettie what I had done, and she would forgive me, and make everything all right.

I could not sleep. My sister was already asleep. She seemed able to go to sleep whenever she wanted to, a skill I envied and did not have.

I left my bedroom.

I loitered at the top of the stairs, listening to the noise of the television coming from downstairs. Then I crept barefoot-silent down the stairs and sat on the third step from the bottom. The door to the television room was half-open, and if I went down another step whoever was watching the television could see me. So I waited there.

I could hear the television voices punctuated by staccato bursts of TV laughter.

And then, over the television voices, adults talking.

Ursula Monkton said, "So, is your wife away every evening?"

My father's voice: "No. She's gone back this evening to organize tomorrow. But from tomorrow it will be weekly. She's raising money for Africa, in the village hall. For drilling wells, and I believe for contraception."

"Well," said Ursula, "I already know all about *that*."

She laughed, a high, tinkling laugh, which sounded friendly and true and real, and had no flapping rags in it. Then she said, "Little pitchers . . . ," and a moment later the door opened the whole way, and Ursula Monkton was looking straight at me. She had redone her makeup, her pale lipstick and her big eyelashes.

"Go to bed," she said. "Now."

"I want to talk to my dad," I said, without hope. She said nothing, just smiled, with no warmth in it, and no love, and I went back up the stairs, and climbed into my bed, and lay in the darkened bedroom until I gave up on sleeping, and then sleep enveloped me when I was not expecting it, and I slept without comfort.

VII.

The next day was bad.

My parents had both left the house before I woke.

It had turned cold, and the sky was a bleak and charmless gray. I went through my parents' bedroom to the balcony that ran along the length of their bedroom and my-sister's-and-mine, and I stood on the long balcony and I prayed to the sky that Ursula Monkton would have tired of this game, and that I would not see her again.

Ursula Monkton was waiting for me at the bottom of the stairs when I went down.

"Same rules as yesterday, little pitcher," she said. "You can't leave the property. If you try, I will lock you in your bedroom for the rest of the day, and when your parents come home I will tell them you did something disgusting."

"They won't believe you."

She smiled sweetly. "Are you sure? If I tell them you pulled out your little willy and widdled all over the kitchen floor, and I had to mop it up and disinfect it? I think they'll believe me. I'll be very convincing."

I went out of the house and down to my laboratory. I ate all the fruit that I had hidden there the day before. I read *Sandie Sees It Through*, another of my mother's books. Sandie was a plucky but poor schoolgirl who was accidentally sent to a posh school, where everybody hated her. In the end she exposed the Geography Teacher as an

International Bolshevik, who had tied the real Geography Teacher
up. The climax was in the school assembly, when Sandie bravely
got up and made a speech which began, "I know I should not have
been sent here. It was only an error in paperwork that sent me here
and sent Sandy spelled with a Y to the town grammar school. But
I thank Providence that I came here. Because Miss Streebling is not
who she claims to be."

In the end Sandie was embraced by the people who had hated her.

My father came home early from work—earlier than I remembered seeing him home in years.

I wanted to talk to him, but he was never alone.

I watched them from the branch of my beech tree.

First he showed Ursula Monkton around the gardens, proudly
showing her the rosebushes and the blackcurrant bushes and the
cherry trees and the azaleas as if he had had anything to do with
them, as if they had not been put in place and tended by Mr. Wollery
for fifty years before ever we had bought the house.

She laughed at all his jokes. I could not hear what he was saying,
but I could see the crooked smile he had when he knew he was saying
something funny.

She was standing too close to him. Sometimes he would rest his
hand on her shoulder, in a friendly sort of way. It worried me that
he was standing so close to her. He didn't know what she was. She
was a monster, and he just thought she was a normal person, and he
was being nice to her. She was wearing different clothes today: a gray
skirt, of the kind they called a midi, and a pink blouse.

On any other day if I had seen my father walking around the
garden, I would have run over to him. But not that day. I was scared
that he would be angry, or that Ursula Monkton would say something to make him angry with me.

I became terrified of him when he was angry. His face (angular and usually affable) would grow red, and he would shout, shout so loudly and furiously that it would, literally, paralyze me. I would not be able to think.

He never hit me. He did not believe in hitting. He would tell us how his father had hit him, how his mother had chased him with a broom, how he was better than that. When he got angry enough to shout at me he would occasionally remind me that he did not hit me, as if to make me grateful. In the school stories I read, misbehavior often resulted in a caning, or the slipper, and then was forgiven and done, and I would sometimes envy those fictional children the cleanness of their lives.

I did not want to approach Ursula Monkton: I did not want to risk making my father angry with me.

I wondered if this would be a good time to try to leave the property, to head down the lane, but I was certain that if I did I would look up to see my father's angry face beside Ursula Monkton's, all pretty and smug.

So I simply watched them from the huge branch of the beech tree. When they walked out of sight, behind the azalea bushes, I clambered down the rope ladder, went up into the house, up to the balcony, and I watched them from there. It was a gray day, but there were butter-yellow daffodils everywhere, and narcissi in profusion, with their pale outer petals and their dark orange trumpets. My father picked a handful of narcissi and gave them to Ursula Monkton, who laughed, and said something, then made a curtsey. He bowed in return, and said something that made her laugh. I thought he must have proclaimed himself her Knight in Shining Armor, or something like that.

I wanted to shout down to him, to warn him that he was giving flowers to a monster, but I did not. I just stood on the balcony and watched, and they did not look up and they did not see me.

My book of Greek myths had told me that the narcissi were named after a beautiful young man, so lovely that he had fallen in love with himself. He saw his reflection in a pool of water, and would not leave it, and, eventually, he died, so that the gods were forced to transform him into a flower. In my mind, when I had read this, I had imagined that a narcissus must be the most beautiful flower in the world. I was disappointed when I learned that it was just a less impressive daffodil.

My sister came out of the house and went over to them. My father picked her up and swung her in the air. They all walked inside together, my father with my sister holding on to his neck, and Ursula Monkton, her arms filled with yellow and white flowers. I watched them. I watched as my father's free hand, the one not holding my sister, went down and rested, casually, proprietarily, on the swell of Ursula Monkton's midi skirted bottom.

I would react differently to that now. At the time, I do not believe I thought anything of it at all. I was seven.

I climbed up into my bedroom window, easy to reach from the balcony, and down onto my bed, where I read a book about a girl who stayed in the Channel Islands and defied the Nazis because she would not abandon her pony.

And while I read, I thought, *Ursula Monkton cannot keep me here forever. Soon enough——in a few days at the most——someone will take me into town, or away from here, and then I will go to the farm at the bottom of the lane, and I will tell Lettie Hempstock what I did.*

Then I thought, *Suppose Ursula Monkton only needs a couple of days.* And that scared me.

Ursula Monkton made meatloaf for dinner that evening, and I would not eat it. I was determined not to eat anything she had made or cooked or touched. My father was not amused.

"But I don't want it," I told him. "I'm not hungry."

It was Wednesday, and my mother was attending her meeting, to raise money so that people in Africa who needed water could drill wells, in the village hall of the next village down the road. She had posters that she would put up, diagrams of wells, and photographs of smiling people. At the dinner table were my sister, my father, Ursula Monkton, and me.

"It's good, it's good for you, and it's tasty," said my father. "And we do not waste food in this house."

"I said I wasn't hungry."

I had lied. I was so hungry it hurt.

"Then just try a little nibble," he said. "It's your favorite. Meat-loaf and mashed potatoes and gravy. You love them."

There was a children's table in the kitchen, where we ate when my parents had friends over, or would be eating late. But that night we were at the adult table. I preferred the children's table. I felt invisible there. Nobody watched me eat.

Ursula Monkton sat next to my father and stared at me, with a tiny smile at the corner of her lips.

I knew I should shut up, be silent, be sullen. But I couldn't help myself. I had to tell my father why I did not want to eat.

"I won't eat anything she made," I told him. "I don't like her."

"You will eat your food," said my father. "You will at least try it. And apologize to Miss Monkton."

"I won't."

"He doesn't have to," said Ursula Monkton sympathetically, and she looked at me, and she smiled. I do not think that either of the other two people at the table noticed that she was smiling with amusement, or that there was nothing sympathetic in her expression, or her smile, or her rotting-cloth eyes.

"I'm afraid he does," said my father. His voice was just a little louder, and his face was just a little redder. "I won't have him cheeking you like that." Then, to me, "Give me one good reason, just one, why you won't apologize and why you won't eat the lovely food that Ursula prepared for us."

I did not lie well. I told him.

"Because she's not human," I said. "She's a monster. She's a . . ." What had the Hempstocks called her kind of thing? "She's a *flea*."

My father's cheeks were burning red, now, and his lips were thin. He said, "Outside. Into the hall. This minute."

My heart sank inside me. I climbed down from my stool and followed him out into the corridor. It was dark in the hallway: the only light came from the kitchen, a sheet of clear glass above the door. He looked down at me. "You will go back into the kitchen. You will apologize to Miss Monkton. You will finish your plate of food, then, quietly and politely, you will go straight upstairs to bed."

"No," I told him. "I won't."

I bolted, ran down the hallway, round the corner, and I pounded up the stairs. My father, I had no doubt, would come after me. He was twice my size, and fast, but I did not have to keep going for long. There was only one room in that house that I could lock, and it was there that I was headed, left at the top of the stairs and along the hall to the end. I reached the bathroom ahead of my father. I slammed the door, and I pushed the little silver bolt closed.

He had not chased me. Perhaps he thought it was beneath his dignity, chasing a child. But in a few moments I heard his fist slam, and then his voice saying, "Open this door."

I didn't say anything. I sat on the plush toilet seat cover and I hated him almost as much as I hated Ursula Monkton.

The door banged again, harder this time. "If you don't open this door," he said, loud enough to make sure I heard it through the door, "I'm breaking it down."

Could he do that? I didn't know. The door was locked. Locked doors stopped people coming in. A locked door meant that you were in there, and when people wanted to come into the bathroom they would jiggle the door, and it wouldn't open, and they would say "Sorry!" or shout "Are you going to be long?" and—

The door exploded inward. The little silver bolt hung off the door frame, all bent and broken, and my father stood in the doorway, filling it, his eyes huge and white, his cheeks burning with fury.

He said, "Right."

That was all he said, but his hand held my left upper arm in a grip I could never have broken. I wondered what he would do now. Would he, finally, hit me, or send me to my room, or shout at me so loudly that I would wish I were dead?

He did none of those things.

He pulled me over to the bathtub. He leaned over, pushed the white rubber plug into the plug hole. Then he turned on the cold tap. Water gushed out, splashing the white enamel, then, steadily and slowly, it filled the bath.

The water ran noisily.

My father turned to the open door. "I can deal with this," he said to Ursula Monkton.

She stood in the doorway, holding my sister's hand, and she looked concerned and gentle, but there was triumph in her eyes.

"Close the door," said my father. My sister started whimpering, but Ursula Monkton closed the door, as best she could, for one of the hinges did not fit properly, and the broken bolt stopped the door closing all the way.

It was just me and my father. His cheeks had gone from red to

white, and his lips were pressed together, and I did not know what
he was going to do, or why he was running a bath, but I was scared,
so scared.

"I'll apologize," I told him. "I'll say sorry. I didn't mean what I
said. She's not a monster. She's . . . she's pretty."

He didn't say anything in response. The bath was full, and he
turned the cold tap off.

Then, swiftly, he picked me up. He put his huge hands under
my armpits, swung me up with ease, so I felt like I weighed nothing
at all.

I looked at him, at the intent expression on his face. He had
taken off his jacket before he came upstairs. He was wearing a light
blue shirt and a maroon paisley tie. He pulled off his watch on its
expandable strap, dropped it onto the window ledge.

Then I realized what he was going to do, and I kicked out, and I
flailed at him, neither of which actions had any effect of any kind as
he plunged me down into the cold water.

I was horrified, but it was initially the horror of something happening against the established order of things. I was fully dressed.
That was wrong. I had my sandals on. That was wrong. The bathwater was cold, so cold and so wrong. That was what I thought,
initially, as he pushed me into the water, and then he pushed further,
pushing my head and shoulders beneath the chilly water, and the
horror changed its nature. I thought, *I'm going to die.*

And, thinking that, I was determined to live.

I flailed with my hands, trying to find something to hold on to,
but there was nothing to grab, only the slippery sides of the bath I'd
bathed in for the last two years. (I had read many books in that bath.
It was one of my safe places. And now, I had no doubt, I was going
to die there.)

I opened my eyes, beneath the water, and I saw it dangling there, in front of my face: my chance for life, and I clutched it with both hands: my father's tie.

I held it tightly, pulled myself up as he pushed me down, gripping it for life itself, pulling my face up and out of that frigid water, holding on to his tie so tightly that he could no longer push my head and shoulders back into the bath without going in himself.

My face was now out of the water, and I clamped my teeth into his tie, just below the knot.

We struggled. I was soaked, took some small pleasure in the knowledge that he was soaked as well, his blue shirt clinging to his huge form.

Now he pushed me down again, but fear of death gives us strength: my hands and my teeth were clamped to his tie, and he could not break his grip on them without hitting me.

My father did not hit me.

He straightened up, and I was pulled up with him, soaked and spluttering and angry and crying and scared. I let go of his tie with my teeth, still held on with my hands.

He said, "You ruined my tie. Let go." The tie knot had tightened to pea size, the lining of the tie was dangling damply outside of it. He said, "You should be glad that your mother isn't here."

I let go, dropped to the puddled bathroom lino. I took a step backward, toward the toilet. He looked down at me. Then he said, "Go to your bedroom. I don't want to see you again tonight."

I went to my room.

VIII.

I was shivering convulsively and I was wet through and I was cold, very cold. It felt like all my heat had been stolen. The wet clothes clung to my flesh and dripped cold water onto the floor. With every step I took my sandals made comical squelching noises, and water oozed from the little diamond-shaped holes on the top of the sandals.

I pulled all of my clothes off, and I left them in a sopping heap on the tiles by the fireplace, where they began to puddle. I took the box of matches from the mantelpiece, turned on the gas tap and lit the flame in the gas fire.

(I am staring at a pond, remembering things that are hard to believe. Why do I find the hardest thing for me to believe, looking back, is that a girl of five and a boy of seven had a gas fire in their bedroom?)

There were no towels in the room, and I stood there, wet, wondering how to dry myself off. I took the thin counterpane that covered my bed, wiped myself off with it, then put on my pajamas. They were red nylon, shiny and striped, with a black plasticized burn mark on the left sleeve, where I had leaned too close to the gas fire once, and the pajama arm caught alight, although by some miracle I had not burned my arm.

There was a dressing gown that I almost never used hanging on the back of the bedroom door, its shadow perfectly positioned to cast nightmare shadows on the wall when the hall light was on and the door was open. I put it on.

The bedroom door opened, and my sister came in to get the nightdress from under her pillow. She said, "You've been so naughty that I'm not even allowed to be in the room with you. I get to sleep in Mummy and Daddy's bed tonight. And Daddy says I can watch the *television*."

There was an old television in a brown wooden cabinet in the corner of my parents' bedroom that was almost never turned on. The vertical hold was unreliable, and the fuzzy black-and-white picture had a tendency to stream, in a slow ribbon: people's heads vanished off the bottom of the screen as their feet descended, in a stately fashion, from the top.

"I don't care," I told her.

"Daddy said you ruined his tie. And he's all wet," said my sister, with satisfaction in her voice.

Ursula Monkton was at the bedroom door. "We don't talk to him," she told my sister. "We won't talk to him again until he's allowed to rejoin the family."

My sister slipped out, heading to the next room, my parents' room. "You aren't in my family," I told Ursula Monkton. "When Mummy comes back, I'll tell her what Daddy did."

"She won't be home for another two hours," said Ursula Monkton. "And what can you say to her that will do anything? She backs up your father in everything, doesn't she?"

She did. They always presented a perfectly united front.

"Don't cross me," said Ursula Monkton. "I have things to do here, and you are getting in my way. Next time it will be so much worse. Next time, I lock you in the attic."

"I'm not afraid of you," I told her. I was afraid of her, more afraid than I had ever been of anything.

"It's hot in here," she told me, and smiled. She walked over to the gas fire, reached down, turned it off, took the matches from the mantel.

I said, "You're still just a flea."

She stopped smiling. She reached up to the lintel above the door, higher than any child could reach, and she pulled down the key that rested there. She walked out of the room, and closed the door. I heard the key turn, heard the lock engage and click.

I could hear television voices coming from the room next door. I heard the hallway door close, cutting off the two bedrooms from the rest of the house, and I knew that Ursula Monkton was going downstairs. I went over to the lock, and squinted through it. I had learned from a book that I could use a pencil to push a key through a keyhole onto a sheet of paper beneath, and free myself that way . . . but the keyhole was empty.

I cried then, cold and still damp, in that bedroom, cried with pain and anger and terror, cried safely in the knowledge that no one would come in and see me, that no one would tease me for crying, as they teased any boys at my school who were unwise enough to give way to tears.

I heard the gentle patter of raindrops against the glass of my bedroom window, and even that brought me no joy.

I cried until I was all cried out. Then I breathed in huge gulps of air, and I thought, Ursula Monkton, flapping canvas monster, worm and flea, would get me if I tried to leave the property. I knew that.

But Ursula Monkton had locked me in. She would not expect me to leave now.

And, perhaps, if I was lucky, she might be distracted.

I opened the bedroom window, and listened to the night. The gentle rain made a noise that was almost a rustling. It was a cold night, and I was already chilled. My sister was in the room next door, watching something on the television. She would not hear me.

I went over to the door, and turned off the light.

I walked through the dark bedroom, and climbed back on the bed.

I'm in my bed, I thought. *I'm lying in my bed, thinking about how upset I am. Soon, I'll fall asleep. I'm in my bed, and I know she's won, and if she checks up on me I'm in my bed, asleep.*

I'm in my bed and it's time for me to sleep now . . . I can't even keep my eyes open. I'm fast asleep. Fast asleep in my bed . . .

I stood on the bed, and climbed out of the window. I hung for a moment, then let myself drop, as quietly as I could, onto the balcony. That was the easy bit.

Growing up, I took so many cues from books. They taught me most of what I knew about what people did, about how to behave. They were my teachers and my advisors. In books, boys climbed trees, so I climbed trees, sometimes very high, always scared of falling. In books, people climbed up and down drainpipes to get in and out of houses, so I climbed up and down drainpipes too. They were the heavy iron drainpipes of old, clamped to the brick, not today's lightweight plastic affairs.

I had never climbed down a drainpipe in the dark, or in the rain, but I knew where the footholds were. I knew also that the biggest challenge would not be falling, a twenty-foot tumble down into the wet flower bed; it was that the drainpipe I was climbing down went past the television room, downstairs, in which, I had no doubt, Ursula Monkton and my father would be watching television.

I tried not to think.

I climbed over the brick wall that edged the balcony, reached out until I felt the iron drainpipe, cold and slick with rain. I held on to it, then took one large step toward it, letting my bare feet come to rest on the metal clamp that encircled the drainpipe, fixing it sturdily to the brick.

I went down, a step at a time, imagining myself Batman, imagining myself a hundred heroes and heroines of school romances, then, remembering myself, I imagined that I was a drop of rain on the wall, a brick, a tree. *I am on my bed*, I thought. I was not here, with the light of the TV room, uncurtained, spilling out below me, making the rain that fell past the window into a series of glittering lines and streaks.

Don't look at me, I thought. *Don't look out of the window.*

I inched down. Usually I would have stepped from the drainpipe over to the TV room's outer window ledge, but that was out of the question. Warily, I lowered myself another few inches, leaned further back into the shadows and away from the light, and I stole a terrified glance into the room, expecting to see my father and Ursula Monkton staring back at me.

The room was empty.

The lights were on, the television on as well, but nobody was sitting on the sofa and the door to the downstairs hallway was open.

I took an easy step down onto the window ledge, hoping against all hope that neither of them would come back in and see me, then I let myself drop from the ledge into the flower bed. The wet earth was soft against my feet.

I was going to run, just run, but there was a light on in the drawing room, where we children never went, the oak-paneled room kept only for best and for special occasions.

The curtains were drawn. The curtains were green velvet, lined with white, and the light that escaped them, where they had not been closed all the way, was golden and soft.

I walked over to the window. The curtains were not completely closed. I could see into the room, see what was immediately in front of me.

I was not sure what I was looking at. My father had Ursula Monkton pressed up against the side of the big fireplace in the far wall. He had his back to me. She did too, her hands pressed against the huge, high mantelpiece. He was hugging her from behind. Her midi skirt was hiked up around her waist.

I did not know exactly what they were doing, and I did not really care, not at that moment. All that mattered was that Ursula Monkton had her attention on something that was not me, and I turned away from the gap in the curtains and the light and the house, and I fled, barefoot, into the rainy dark.

It was not pitch-black. It was the kind of cloudy night where the clouds seem to gather up light from distant streetlights and houses below, and throw it back at the earth. I could see enough, once my eyes adjusted. I made it to the bottom of the garden, past the compost heap and the grass cuttings, then down the hill to the lane. Brambles and thorns stuck my feet and pricked my legs, but I kept running.

I went over the low metal fence, into the lane. I was off our property and it felt as if a headache I had not known that I had had suddenly lifted. I whispered, urgently, "Lettie? Lettie Hempstock?" and I thought, *I'm in bed. I'm dreaming all this. Such vivid dreams. I am in my bed*, but I did not believe that Ursula Monkton was thinking about me just then.

As I ran, I thought of my father, his arms around the housekeeper-who-wasn't, kissing her neck, and then I saw his face through the chilly bathwater as he held me under, and now I was no longer scared by what had happened in the bathroom; now I was scared by what it meant that my father was kissing the neck of Ursula Monkton, that his hands had lifted her midi skirt above her waist.

My parents were a unit, inviolate. The future had suddenly become unknowable: anything could happen: the train of my life had jumped the rails and headed off across the fields and was coming down the lane with me, then.

The flints of the lane hurt my feet as I ran, but I did not care. Soon enough, I was certain, the thing that was Ursula Monkton would be done with my father. Perhaps they would go upstairs to check on me together. She would find that I was gone and she would come after me.

I thought, *If they come after me, they will be in a car.* I looked for a gap in the hedgerow on either side of the lane. I spotted a wooden stile and clambered over it, and kept running across the meadow, heart pounding like the biggest loudest drum there was or had ever been, barefoot, with my pajamas and my dressing gown all soaked below the knee and clinging. I ran, not caring about the cow-pats. The meadow was easier on my feet than the flint lane had been. I was happier, and I felt more real, running on the grass.

Thunder rumbled behind me, although I had seen no lightning. I climbed a fence, and my feet sank into the soft earth of a freshly plowed field. I stumbled across it, falling sometimes, but I kept going. Over a stile and into the next field, this one unplowed, and I crossed it, keeping close to the hedge, scared of being too far out in the open.

The lights of a car came down the lane, sudden and blinding. I froze where I was, closed my eyes, imagined myself asleep in my bed. The car drove past without slowing, and I caught a glimpse of its rear red lights as it moved away from me: a white van, that I thought belonged to the Anders family.

Still, it made the lane seem less safe, and now I cut away across the meadow. I reached the next field, saw it was only divided from the one I was in by thin lengths of wire, easy to duck beneath, not even barbed wire, so I reached out my arm and pushed a bare wire up to make room to squeeze under, and—

It was as if I had been thumped, and thumped hard, in the chest. My arm, where it had grasped the wire of the fence, was convulsed, and my palm was burning as if I had just slammed my funny bone into a wall.

I let go of the electric fence and stumbled back. I could not run any longer, but I hurried in the wind and the rain and the darkness along the side of the fence, careful now not to touch it, until I reached a five-bar gate. I went over the gate, and across the field, heading to the deeper darkness at the far end—trees, I thought, and woodland—and I did not go too close to the edge of the field in case there was another electric fence waiting for me.

I hesitated, uncertain where to go next. As if in answer, the world was illuminated, for a moment, but I only needed a moment, by lightning. I saw a wooden stile, and I ran for it.

Over the stile. I came down into a clump of nettles, I knew, as the hot-cold pricking burning covered my exposed ankles and the tops of my feet, but I ran again, now, ran as best I could. I hoped I was still heading for the Hempstocks' farm. I had to be. I crossed one more field before I realized that I no longer knew where the lane was, or for that matter, where I was. I knew only that the Hempstocks' farm was at the end of my lane, but I was lost in a dark field, and the thunderclouds had lowered, and the night was so dark, and it was still raining, even if it was not raining hard yet, and now my imagination filled the darkness with wolves and ghosts. I wanted to stop imagining, to stop thinking, but I could not.

And behind the wolves and the ghosts and the trees that walked, there was Ursula Monkton, telling me that the next time I disobeyed her it would be so much worse for me, that she would lock me in the attic.

I was not brave. I was running away from everything, and I was cold, and wet and lost.

I shouted, at the top of my voice, "Lettie? Lettie Hempstock! Hello?" but there was no reply, and I had not expected one.

The thunder grumbled and rumbled into a low continuous roar, a lion pushed into irritability, and the lightning was flashing and flickering like a malfunctioning fluorescent tube. In the flickers of light, I could see that the area of field I was in came to a point, with hedges on both sides, and no way through. I could see no gate, and no stile other than the one I had come in through, at the far end of the field.

Something crackled.

I looked up at the sky. I had seen lightning in films on the television, long jagged forks of light across the clouds. But the lightning I had seen until now with my own eyes was simply a white flash from above, like the flash of a camera, burning the world in a strobe of visibility. What I saw in the sky then was not that.

It was not forked lightning either.

It came and it went, a writhing, burning blue-whiteness in the sky. It died back and then it flared up, and its flares and flickers illuminated the meadow, made it something I could see. The rain pattered hard, and it whipped against my face, moved in a moment from a drizzle to a downpour. In seconds my dressing gown was soaked through. But in the light I saw—or thought I saw—an opening in the hedgerow to my right, and I walked, for I could no longer run, not any longer, as fast as I could, toward it, hoping it was something real. My wet gown flapped in the gusting wind, and the sound of the flapping cloth horrified me.

I did not look up in the sky. I did not look behind me.

But I could see the far end of the field, and there was indeed a space between the hedgerows. I had almost reached it when a voice said,

"I thought I told you to stay in your room. And now I find you sneaking around like a drowned sailor."

I turned, looked behind me, saw nothing at all. There was nobody there.

Then I looked up.

The thing that called itself Ursula Monkton hung in the air, about twenty feet above me, and lightnings crawled and flickered in the sky behind her. She was not flying. She was floating, weightless as a balloon, although the sharp gusts of wind did not move her.

Wind howled and whipped at my face. The distant thunder roared and smaller thunders crackled and spat, and she spoke quietly, but I could hear every word she said as distinctly as if she were whispering into my ears.

"Oh, sweety-weety-pudding-and-pie, you are in so much trouble."

She was smiling, the hugest, toothiest grin I had ever seen on a human face, but she did not look amused.

I had been running from her through the darkness for, what, half an hour? An hour? I wished I had stayed on the lane and not tried to cut across the fields. I would have been at the Hempstocks' farm by now. Instead, I was lost and I was trapped.

Ursula Monkton came lower. Her pink blouse was open and unbuttoned. She wore a white bra. Her midi skirt flapped in the wind, revealing her calves. She did not appear to be wet, despite the storm. Her clothes, her face, her hair, were perfectly dry.

She was floating above me, now, and she reached out her hands.

Every move she made, everything she did, was strobed by the tame lightnings that flickered and writhed about her. Her fingers opened like flowers in a speeded-up film, and I knew that she was playing with me, and I knew what she wanted me to do, and I hated myself for not standing my ground, but I did what she wanted: I ran.

I was a little thing that amused her. She was playing, just as I had seen Monster, the big orange tomcat, play with a mouse—letting it go, so that it would run, and then pouncing, and batting it down with a paw. But the mouse still ran, and I had no choice, and I ran too.

I ran for the break in the hedge, as fast as I could, stumbling and hurting and wet.

Her voice was in my ears as I ran.

"I told you I was going to lock you in the attic, didn't I? And I will. Your daddy likes me now. He'll do whatever I say. Perhaps from now on, every night, he'll come up the ladder and let you out of the attic. He'll make you climb down from the attic. Down the ladder. And every night, he'll drown you in the bath, he'll plunge you into the cold, cold water. I'll let him do it every night until it bores me, and then I'll tell him not to bring you back, to simply push you under the water until you stop moving and until there's nothing but darkness and water in your lungs. I'll have him leave you in the cold bath, and you'll never move again. And every night I'll kiss him and kiss him . . ."

I was through the gap in the hedgerow, and running on soft grass.

The crackle of the lightning, and a strange sharp, metallic smell, were so close they made my skin prickle. Everything around me got brighter and brighter, illuminated by the flickering blue-white light.

"And when your daddy finally leaves you in the bath for good, you'll be happy," whispered Ursula Monkton, and I imagined that I could feel her lips brushing my ears. "Because you won't like it in the attic. Not just because it's dark up there, with the spiders, and the ghosts. But because I'm going to bring my friends. You can't see them in the daylight, but they'll be in the attic with you, and you won't enjoy them at all. They don't like little boys, my friends. They'll pretend to be spiders as big as dogs. Old clothes with nothing inside that tug at you and never let you go. The inside of your head. And when you're in the attic there will be no books, and no stories, not ever again."

I had not imagined it. Her lips had brushed my ear. She was floating in the air beside me, so her head was beside mine, and when she caught me looking at her she smiled her pretend-smile, and I could not run any longer. I could barely move. I had a stitch in my side, and I could not catch my breath, and I was done.

My legs gave way beneath me, and I stumbled and fell, and this time I did not get up.

I felt heat on my legs, and I looked down to see a yellow stream coming from the front of my pajama trousers. I was seven years old, no longer a little child, but I was wetting myself with fear, like a baby, and there was nothing I could do about it, while Ursula Monkton hung in the air a few feet above me and watched, dispassionately.

The hunt was done.

She stood up straight in the air, three feet above the ground. I was sprawled beneath her, on my back, in the wet grass. She began to descend, slowly, inexorably, like a person on a broken television screen.

Something touched my left hand. Something soft. It nosed my hand, and I looked over, fearing a spider as big as a dog. Illuminated by the lightnings that writhed about Ursula Monkton, I saw a patch of darkness beside my hand. A patch of darkness with a white spot over one ear. I picked the kitten up in my hand, and brought it to my heart, and I stroked it.

I said, "I won't come with you. You can't make me." I sat up, because I felt less vulnerable sitting, and the kitten curled and made itself comfortable in my hand.

"Pudding-and-pie boy," said Ursula Monkton. Her feet touched

the ground. She was illuminated by her own lightnings, like a paint-
ing of a woman in grays and greens and blues, and not a real woman
at all. "You're just a little boy. I'm a grown-up. I was an adult when
your world was a ball of molten rock. I can do whatever I wish to
you. Now, stand up. I'm taking you home."

The kitten, which was burrowing into my chest with its face,
made a high-pitched noise, not a mew. I turned, looking away from
Ursula Monkton, looking behind me.

The girl who was walking toward us, across the field, wore a
shiny red raincoat, with a hood, and a pair of black Wellington
boots that seemed too big for her. She walked out of the darkness,
unafraid. She looked up at Ursula Monkton.

"Get off my land," said Lettie Hempstock.

Ursula Monkton took a step backwards and she rose, at the same
time, so she hung in the air above us. Lettie Hempstock reached out
to me, without glancing down at where I sat, and she took my hand,
twining her fingers into mine.

"I'm not touching your land," said Ursula Monkton. "Go away,
little girl."

"You are on my land," said Lettie Hempstock.

Ursula Monkton smiled, and the lightnings wreathed and
writhed about her. She was power incarnate, standing in the crack-
ling air. She was the storm, she was the lightning, she was the adult
world with all its power and all its secrets and all its foolish casual
cruelty. She winked at me.

I was a seven-year-old boy, and my feet were scratched and bleed-
ing. I had just wet myself. And the thing that floated above me was
huge and greedy, and it wanted to take me to the attic, and, when it
tired of me, it would make my daddy kill me.

Lettie Hempstock's hand in my hand made me braver. But Lettie was just a girl, even if she was a big girl, even if she was eleven, even if she had been eleven for a very long time. Ursula Monkton was an adult. It did not matter, at that moment, that she was every monster, every witch, every nightmare made flesh. She was also an adult, and when adults fight children, adults always win.

Lettie said, "You should go back where you came from in the first place. It's not healthy for you to be here. For your own good, go back."

A noise in the air, a horrible, twisted scratching noise, filled with pain and with wrongness, a noise that set my teeth on edge and made the kitten, its front paws resting on my chest, stiffen and its fur prickle. The little thing twisted and clawed up onto my shoulder, and it hissed and it spat. I looked up at Ursula Monkton. It was only when I saw her face that I knew what the noise was.

Ursula Monkton was laughing.

"Go back? When your people ripped the hole in Forever, I seized my chance. I could have ruled worlds, but I followed you, and I waited, and I had patience. I knew that sooner or later the bounds would loosen, that I would walk the true Earth, beneath the Sun of Heaven." She was not laughing now. "Everything here is so weak, little girl. Everything breaks so easily. They want such simple things. I will take all I want from this world, like a child stuffing its fat little face with blackberries from a bush."

I did not let go of Lettie's hand, not this time. I stroked the kitten, whose needle-claws were digging into my shoulder, and I was bitten for my trouble, but the kitten's bite was not hard, just scared.

Her voice came from all around us, as the storm-wind gusted. "You kept me away from here for a long time. But then you brought me a door, and I used him to carry me out of my cell. And what can you do now that I am out?"

Lettie didn't seem angry. She thought about it, then she said, "I could make you a new door. Or, better still, I could get Granny to send you across the ocean, all the way to wherever you came from in the beginning."

Ursula Monkton spat onto the grass, and a tiny ball of flame sputtered and fizzed on the ground, where the spit had fallen.

"Give me the boy," was all she said. "He belongs to me. I came here inside him. I own him."

"You don't own nuffink, you don't," said Lettie Hempstock, angrily. "'Specially not him." Lettie helped me to my feet, and she stood behind me and put her arms around me. We were two children in a field in the night. Lettie held me, and I held the kitten, while above us and all around us a voice said,

"What will you do? Take him home with you? This world is a world of rules, little girl. He belongs to his parents, after all. Take him away and his parents will come to bring him home, and his parents belong to me."

"I'm all bored of you now," said Lettie Hempstock. "I gived you a chance. You're on my land. Go away."

As she said that, my skin felt like it did when I'd rubbed a balloon on my sweater, then touched it to my face and hair. Everything prickled and tickled. My hair was soaked, but even wet, it felt like it was starting to stand on end.

Lettie Hempstock held me tightly. "Don't worry," she whispered, and I was going to say something, to ask why I shouldn't worry, what I had to be afraid of, when the field we were standing in began to glow.

It glowed golden. Every blade of grass glowed and glimmered, every leaf on every tree. Even the hedges were glowing. It was a warm light. It seemed, to my eyes, as if the soil beneath the grass had transmuted from base matter into pure light, and in the golden glow of the meadow the blue-white lightnings that still crackled around Ursula Monkton seemed much less impressive.

Ursula Monkton rose unsteadily, as if the air had just become hot and was carrying her upwards. Then Lettie Hempstock whispered old words into the world and the meadow exploded into a golden light. I saw Ursula Monkton swept up and away, although I felt no wind, but there had to be a wind, for she was flailing and tipping like a dead leaf in a gale. I watched her tumble into the night, and then Ursula Monkton and her lightnings were gone.

"Come on," said Lettie Hempstock. "We should get you in front of a kitchen fire. And a hot bath. You'll catch your death." She let go of my hand, stopped hugging me, stepped back. The golden glow dimmed, so slowly, and then it was gone, leaving only vanishing glimmers and twinkles in the bushes, like the final moments of the fireworks on Bonfire Night.

"Is she dead?" I asked.

"No."

"Then she'll come back. And you'll get in trouble."

"That's as may be," said Lettie. "Are you hungry?"

She asked me, and I knew that I was. I had forgotten, somehow, but now I remembered. I was so hungry it hurt.

"Let's see . . ." Lettie was talking as she led me through the fields. "You're wet through. We'll need to get you something to wear. I'll have a look in the chest of drawers in the green bedroom. I think Cousin Japeth left some of his clothes there when he went off to fight in the Mouse Wars. He wasn't much bigger than you."

The kitten was licking my fingers with a small, rough tongue.

"I found a kitten," I said.

"I can see that. She must have followed you back from the fields where you pulled her up."

"This is *that* kitten? The same one that I picked?"

"Yup. Did she tell you her name, yet?"

"No. Do they do that?"

"Sometimes. If you listen."

I saw the lights of the Hempstocks' farm in front of us, welcoming, and I was cheered, although I could not understand how we had got from the field we were in to the farmhouse so quickly.

"You were lucky," said Lettie. "Fifteen feet further back, and the field belongs to Colin Anders."

"You would have come anyway," I told her. "You would have saved me."

She squeezed my arm with her hand but she said nothing.

I said, "Lettie. I don't want to go home." That was not true. I wanted to go home more than anything, just not to the place I had fled that night. I wanted to go back to the home I had lived in before the opal miner had killed himself in our little white Mini, or before he had run over my kitten.

The ball of dark fur pressed itself into my chest, and I wished she was my kitten, and knew that she was not. The rain had become a drizzle once again.

We splashed through deep puddles, Lettie in her Wellington boots, my stinging feet bare. The smell of manure was sharp in the air as we reached the farmyard, and then we walked through a side door and into the huge farmhouse kitchen.

IX.

Lettie's mother was prodding the huge fireplace with a poker, pushing the burning logs together.

Old Mrs. Hempstock was stirring a bulbous pot on the stove with a large wooden spoon. She lifted the spoon to her mouth, blew on it theatrically, sipped from it, pursed her lips, then added a pinch of something and a fistful of something else to it. She turned down the flame. Then she looked at me, from my wet hair to my bare feet, which were blue with cold. As I stood there a puddle began to appear on the flagstone floor around me, and the drips of water from my dressing gown splashed into it.

"Hot bath," said Old Mrs. Hempstock. "Or he'll catch his death."

"That was what I said," said Lettie.

Lettie's mother was already hauling a tin bath from beneath the kitchen table, and filling it with steaming water from the enormous black kettle that hung above the fireplace. Pots of cold water were added until she pronounced it the perfect temperature.

"Right. In you go," said Old Mrs. Hempstock. "Spit-spot."

I looked at her, horrified. Was I going to have to undress in front of people I didn't know?

"We'll wash your clothes, and dry them for you, and mend that dressing gown," said Lettie's mother, and she took the dressing gown from me, and she took the kitten, which I had barely realized I was still holding, and then she walked away.

As quickly as possible I shed my red nylon pajamas—the bottoms were soaked and the legs were now ragged and ripped and would never be whole again. I dipped my fingers into the water, then I climbed in and sat down on the tin floor of the bath in that reassuring kitchen in front of the huge fire, and I leaned back in the hot water. My feet began to throb as they came back to life. I knew that *naked* was wrong, but the Hempstocks seemed indifferent to my nakedness: Lettie was gone, and my pajamas and dressing gown with her; her mother was getting out knives, forks, spoons, little jugs and bigger jugs, carving knives and wooden trenchers, and arranging them about the table.

Old Mrs. Hempstock passed me a mug, filled with soup from the black pot on the stove. "Get that down you. Heat you up from the inside, first."

The soup was rich, and warming. I had never drunk soup in the bath before. It was a perfectly new experience. When I finished the mug I gave it back to her, and in return she passed me a large cake of white soap and a face-flannel and said, "Now get scrubbin'. Rub the life and the warmth back into your bones."

She sat down in a rocking chair on the other side of the fire, and rocked gently, not looking at me.

I felt safe. It was as if the essence of grandmotherliness had been condensed into that one place, that one time. I was not at all afraid of Ursula Monkton, whatever she was, not then. Not there.

Young Mrs. Hempstock opened an oven door and took out a pie, its shiny crust brown and glistening, and put it on the window ledge to cool.

I dried myself off with a towel they brought me, the fire's heat drying me as much as the towel did, then Lettie Hempstock returned and gave me a voluminous white thing, like a girl's nightdress but made of white cotton, with long arms, and a skirt that draped to the floor, and a white cap. I hesitated to put it on until I realized what it was: a nightgown. I had seen pictures of them in books. Wee Willie Winkie ran through the town wearing one in every book of nursery rhymes I had ever owned.

I slipped into it. The nightcap was too big for me, and fell down over my face, and Lettie took it away once more.

Dinner was wonderful. There was a joint of beef, with roast potatoes, golden-crisp on the outside and soft and white inside, buttered greens I did not recognize, although I think now that they might have been nettles, roasted carrots all blackened and sweet (I did not think that I liked cooked carrots, so I nearly did not eat one, but I was brave, and I tried it, and I liked it, and was disappointed in boiled carrots for the rest of my childhood). For dessert there was the pie, stuffed with apples and with swollen raisins and crushed nuts, all topped with a thick yellow custard, creamier and richer than anything I had ever tasted at school or at home.

The kitten slept on a cushion beside the fire, until the end of the meal, when it joined a fog-colored house cat four times its size in a meal of scraps of meat.

While we ate, nothing was said about what had happened to me, or why I was there. The Hempstock ladies talked about the farm—there was the door to the milking shed needed a new coat of paint, a cow named Rhiannon who looked to be getting lame in her left hind leg, the path to be cleared on the way that led down to the reservoir.

"Is it just the three of you?" I asked. "Aren't there any men?"

"Men!" hooted Old Mrs. Hempstock. "I dunno what blessed

good a man would be! Nothing a man could do around this farm that I can't do twice as fast and five times as well."

Lettie said, "We've had men here, sometimes. They come and they go. Right now, it's just us."

Her mother nodded. "They went off to seek their fate and fortune, mostly, the male Hempstocks. There's never any keeping them here when the call comes. They get a distant look in their eyes and then we've lost them, good and proper. Next chance they gets they're off to towns and even cities, and nothing but an occasional postcard to even show they were here at all."

Old Mrs. Hempstock said, "His parents are coming! They're driving here. They just passed Parson's elm tree. The badgers saw them."

"Is she with them?" I asked. "Ursula Monkton?"

"Her?" said Old Mrs. Hempstock, amused. "That thing? Not her."

I thought about it for a moment. "They will make me go back with them, and then she'll lock me in the attic and let my daddy kill me when she gets bored. She said so."

"She may have told you that, ducks," said Lettie's mother, "but she en't going to do it, or anything like it, or my name's not Ginnie Hempstock."

I liked the name Ginnie, but I did not believe her, and I was not reassured. Soon the door to the kitchen would open, and my father would shout at me, or he would wait until we got into the car, and he would shout at me then, and they would take me back up the lane to my house, and I would be lost.

"Let's see," said Ginnie Hempstock. "We could be away when they get here. They could arrive last Tuesday, when there's nobody home."

"Out of the question," said the old woman. "Just complicates things, playing with time . . . We could turn the boy into something else, so they'd never find him, look how hard they might."

I blinked. Was that even possible? I wanted to be turned into something. The kitten had finished its portion of meat-scraps (indeed, it seemed to have eaten more than the house cat) and now it leapt into my lap, and began to wash itself.

Ginnie Hempstock got up and went out of the room. I wondered where she was going.

"We can't turn him into anything," said Lettie, clearing the table of the last of the plates and cutlery. "His parents will get frantic. And if they are being controlled by the flea, she'll just feed the franticness. Next thing you know, we'll have the police dragging the reservoir, looking for him. Or worse. The ocean."

The kitten lay down on my lap and curled up, wrapping around itself until it was nothing more than a flattened circlet of fluffy black fur. It closed its vivid blue eyes, the color of an ocean, and it slept, and it purred.

"Well?" said Old Mrs. Hempstock. "What do you suggest, then?"

Lettie thought, pushing her lips together, moving them over to one side. Her head tipped, and I thought she was running through alternatives. Then her face brightened. "Snip and cut?" she said.

Old Mrs. Hempstock sniffed. "You're a good girl," she said. "I'm not saying you're not. But snippage . . . well, *you* couldn't do that. Not yet. You'd have to cut the edges out exactly, sew them back without the seam showing. And what would you cut out? The flea won't let you snip *her*. She's not in the fabric. She's outside of it."

Ginnie Hempstock returned. She was carrying my old dressing gown. "I put it through the mangle," she said. "But it's still damp. That'll make the edges harder to line up. You don't want to do needlework when it's still damp."

She put the dressing gown down on the table, in front of Old Mrs. Hempstock. Then she pulled out from the front pocket of her apron a pair of scissors, black and old, a long needle, and a spool of red thread.

"*Rowanberry and red thread, stop a witch in her speed,*" I recited. It was something I had read in a book.

"That'd work, and work well," said Lettie, "if there was any witches involved in all this. But there's not."

Old Mrs. Hempstock was examining my dressing gown. It was brown and faded, with a sort of a sepia tartan across it. It had been a present from my father's parents, my grandparents, several birthdays ago, when it had been comically big on me. "Probably . . . ," she said, as if she was talking to herself, "it would be best if your father was happy for you to stay the night here. But for that to happen they couldn't be angry with you, or even worried . . ."

The black scissors were in her hand and already snip-snip-snipping then, when I heard a knock on the front door, and Ginnie Hempstock got up to answer it. She went into the hall and closed the door behind her.

"Don't let them take me," I said to Lettie.

"Hush," she said. "I'm working here, while Grandmother's snipping. You just be sleepy, and at peace. Happy."

I was far from happy, and not in the slightest bit sleepy. Lettie leaned across the table, and she took my hand. "Don't worry," she said.

And with that the door opened, and my father and my mother were in the kitchen. I wanted to hide, but the kitten shifted reassuringly, on my lap, and Lettie smiled at me, a reassuring smile.

"We are looking for our son," my father was telling Mrs. Hempstock, "and we have reason to believe . . ." And even as he was saying that my mother was striding toward me. "*There* he is! Darling, we were worried *silly*!"

"You're in a lot of trouble, young man," said my father.

Snip! Snip! Snip! went the black scissors, and the irregular section of fabric that Old Mrs. Hempstock had been cutting fell to the table.

My parents froze. They stopped talking, stopped moving. My father's mouth was still open, my mother stood on one leg, as unmoving as if she were a shop-window dummy.

"What . . . what did you do to them?" I was unsure whether or not I ought to be upset.

Ginnie Hempstock said, "They're fine. Just a little snipping, then a little sewing and it'll all be good as gold." She reached down to the table, pointed to the scrap of faded dressing gown tartan resting upon it. "*That's* your dad and you in the hallway, and *that's* the bathtub. She's snipped that out. So without any of that, there's no reason for your daddy to be angry with you."

I had not told them about the bathtub. I did not wonder how she knew.

Now the old woman was threading the needle with the red thread. She sighed, theatrically. "Old eyes," she said. "Old eyes." But she licked the tip of the thread and pushed it through the eye of the needle without any apparent difficulty.

"Lettie. You'll need to know what his toothbrush looks like," said the old woman. She began to sew the edges of the dressing gown together with tiny, careful stitches.

"What's your toothbrush look like?" asked Lettie. "Quickly."

"It's green," I said. "Bright green. A sort of appley green. It's not very big. Just a green toothbrush, my size." I wasn't describing it very well, I knew. I pictured it in my head, tried to find something more about it that I could describe, to set it apart from all other toothbrushes. No good. I imagined it, saw it in my mind's eye, with the other toothbrushes in its red-and-white-spotted beaker above the bathroom sink.

"Got it!" said Lettie. "Nice job."

"Very nearly done here," said Old Mrs. Hempstock.

Ginnie Hempstock smiled a huge smile, and it lit up her ruddy round face. Old Mrs. Hempstock picked up the scissors and snipped a final time, and a fragment of red thread fell to the tabletop.

My mother's foot came down. She took a step and then she stopped.

My father said, "Um."

Ginnie said, " . . . and it made our Lettie so happy that your boy would come here and stay the night. It's a bit old-fashioned here, I'm afraid."

The old woman said, "We've got an inside lavvy nowadays. I don't know how much more modern anybody could be. Outside lavvies and chamber pots were good enough for me."

"He ate a fine meal," said Ginnie to me. "Didn't you?"

"There was pie," I told my parents. "For dessert."

My father's brow was creased. He looked confused. Then he put his hand into the pocket of his car coat, and pulled out something long and green, with toilet paper wrapped around the top. "You forgot your toothbrush," he said. "Thought you'd want it."

"Now, if he wants to come home, he can come home," my mother was saying to Ginnie Hempstock. "He went to stay the night at the Kovacses' house a few months ago, and by nine he was calling us to come and get him."

Christopher Kovacs was two years older and a head taller than me, and he lived with his mother in a large cottage opposite the entrance to our lane, by the old green water tower. His mother was divorced. I liked her. She was funny, and drove a VW Beetle, the first I had ever seen. Christopher owned many books I had not read, and was a member of the Puffin Club. I could read his Puffin books, but only if I went to his house. He would never let me borrow them.

There was a bunk bed in Christopher's bedroom, although he was an only child. I was given the bottom bunk, the night I stayed there. Once I was in bed, and Christopher Kovacs's mother had said good night to us and she had turned out the bedroom light and closed the door, he leaned down and began squirting me with a water pistol he had hidden beneath his pillow. I had not known what to do.

"This isn't like when I went to Christopher Kovacs's house," I told my mother, embarrassed. "I *like* it here."

"What *are* you wearing?" She stared at my Wee Willie Winkie nightgown in puzzlement.

Ginnie said, "He had a little accident. He's wearing that while his pajamas are drying."

"Oh. I see," said my mother. "Well, good night, dear. Have a nice time with your new friend." She peered down at Lettie. "What's your name again, dear?"

"Lettie," said Lettie Hempstock.

"Is it short for Letitia?" asked my mother. "I knew a Letitia when I was at university. Of course, everybody called her Lettuce."

Lettie just smiled, and did not say anything at all.

My father put my toothbrush down on the table in front of me. I unwrapped the toilet paper around the head. It was, unmistakably, my green toothbrush. Under his car coat my father was wearing a clean white shirt, and no tie.

I said, "Thank you."

"So," said my mother. "What time should we be by to pick him up in the morning?"

Ginnie smiled even wider. "Oh, Lettie will bring him back to you. We should give them some time to play, tomorrow morning. Now, before you go, I baked some scones this afternoon . . ."

And she put some scones into a paper bag, which my mother

took politely, and Ginnie ushered her and my father out of the door. I held my breath until I heard the sound of the Rover driving away back up the lane.

"What did you do to them?" I asked. And then, "Is this really my toothbrush?"

"That," said Old Mrs. Hempstock, with satisfaction in her voice, "was a very respectable job of snipping and stitching, if you ask me." She held up my dressing gown: I could not see where she had removed a piece, nor where she had stitched it up. It was seamless, the mend invisible. She passed me the scrap of fabric on the table that she had cut. "Here's your evening," she said. "You can keep it, if you wish. But if I were you, I'd burn it."

The rain pattered against the window, and the wind rattled the window frames.

I picked up the jagged-edged sliver of cloth. It was damp. I got up, waking the kitten, who sprang off my lap and vanished into the shadows. I walked over to the fireplace.

"If I burn this," I asked them, "will it have really happened? Will my daddy have pushed me down into the bath? Will I forget it ever happened?"

Ginnie Hempstock was no longer smiling. Now she looked concerned. "What do *you* want?" she asked.

"I *want* to remember," I said. "Because it happened to me. And I'm still me." I threw the little scrap of cloth onto the fire.

There was a crackle and the cloth smoked, then it began to burn.

I was under the water. I was holding on to my father's tie. I thought he was going to kill me . . .

I screamed.

I was lying on the flagstone floor of the Hempstocks' kitchen and I was rolling and screaming. My foot felt like I had trodden,

barefoot, on a burning cinder. The pain was intense. There was another pain, too, deep inside my chest, more distant, not as sharp: a
discomfort, not a burning.

Ginnie was beside me. "What's wrong?"

"My foot. It's on fire. It hurts so much."

She examined it, then licked her finger, touched it to the hole in
my sole from which I had pulled the worm, two days before. There
was a hissing noise, and the pain in my foot began to ease.

"En't never seen one of these before," said Ginnie Hempstock.
"How did you get it?"

"There was a worm inside me," I told her. "That was how it came
with us from the place with the orangey sky. In my foot." And then I
looked at Lettie, who had crouched beside me and was now holding
my hand, and I said, "I brought it back. It was my fault. I'm sorry."

Old Mrs. Hempstock was the last to reach me. She leaned over,
pulled the sole of my foot up and into the light. "Nasty," she said.
"And very clever. She left the hole inside you so she could use it
again. She could have hidden inside you, if she needed to, used you
as a door to go home. No wonder she wanted to keep you in the
attic. So. Let's strike while the iron's hot, as the soldier said when
he entered the laundry." She prodded the hole in my foot with her
finger. It still hurt, but the pain had faded, a little. Now it felt like a
throbbing headache inside my foot.

Something fluttered in my chest, like a tiny moth, and then was still.

Old Mrs. Hempstock said, "Can you be brave?"

I did not know. I did not think so. It seemed to me that all I had
done so far that night was to run from things. The old woman was
holding the needle she had used to sew up my dressing gown, and she
grasped it now, not as if she were going to sew anything with it, but
as if she were planning to stab me.

I pulled my foot back. "What are you going to do?"

Lettie squeezed my hand. "She's going to make the hole go away," she said. "I'll hold your hand. You don't have to look, not if you don't want to."

"It will hurt," I said.

"Stuff and nonsense," said the old woman. She pulled my foot toward her, so the sole was facing her, and stabbed the needle down . . . not into my foot, I realized, but into the hole itself.

It did not hurt.

Then she twisted the needle and pulled it back toward her. I watched, amazed, as something that glistened—it seemed black, at first, then translucent, then reflective like mercury—was pulled out from the sole of my foot, on the end of the needle.

I could feel it leaving my leg—the sensation seemed to travel up all the way inside me, up my leg, through my groin and my stomach and into my chest. I felt it leave me with relief: the burning feeling abated, as did my terror.

My heart pounded strangely.

I watched Old Mrs. Hempstock reel the thing in, and I was still unable, somehow, to entirely make sense of what I was seeing. It was a hole with nothing around it, over two feet long, thinner than an earthworm, like the shed skin of a translucent snake.

And then she stopped reeling it in. "Doesn't want to come out," she said. "It's holding on."

There was a coldness in my heart, as if a chip of ice were lodged there. The old woman gave an expert flick of her wrist, and then the glistening thing was dangling from her needle (I found myself thinking now not of mercury, but of the silvery slime trails that snails leave in the garden), and it no longer went into my foot.

She let go of my sole and I pulled the foot back. The tiny round hole had vanished completely, as if it had never been there.

Old Mrs. Hempstock cackled with glee. "Thinks she's so clever," she said, "leaving her way home inside the boy. Is that clever? I don't think that's clever. I wouldn't give tuppence for the lot of them."

Ginnie Hempstock produced an empty jam jar, and the old woman put the bottom of the dangling thing into it, then raised the jar to hold it. At the end, she slipped the glistening invisible trail off the needle and put the lid on the jam jar with a decisive flick of her bony wrist.

"Ha!" she said. And again, "Ha!"

Lettie said, "Can I see it?" She took the jam jar, held it up to the light. Inside the jar the thing had begun lazily to uncurl. It seemed to be floating, as if the jar had been filled with water. It changed color as it caught the light in different ways, sometimes black, sometimes silver.

An experiment that I had found in a book of things boys could do, and which I had, of course, done: if you take an egg, and blacken it completely with soot from a candle flame, and then put it into a clear container filled with salt water, it will hang in the middle of the water, and it will seem to be silver: a peculiar, artificial silver, that is only a trick of the light. I thought of that egg, then.

Lettie seemed fascinated. "You're right. She left her way home inside him. No wonder she didn't want him to leave."

I said, "I'm sorry I let go of your hand, Lettie."

"Oh, hush," she said. "It's always too late for sorries, but I appreciate the sentiment. And next time, you'll keep hold of my hand no matter what she throws at us."

I nodded. The ice chip in my heart seemed to warm then, and melt, and I began to feel whole and safe once more.

"So," said Ginnie. "We've got her way home. And we've got the boy safe. That's a good night's work or I don't know what is."

"But she's got the boy's parents," said Old Mrs. Hempstock. "And his sister. And we can't just leave her running around. Remem-

ber what happened in Cromwell's day? And before that? When Red
Rufus was running around? Fleas attract varmints." She said it as if
it were a natural law.

"That can wait until the morrow," said Ginnie. "Now, Lettie.
Take the lad and find a room for him to sleep in. He's had a long day."

The black kitten was curled up on the rocking chair beside the
fireplace. "Can I bring the kitten with me?"

"If you don't," said Lettie, "she'll just come and find you."

Ginnie produced two candlesticks, the kind with big round handles, each one with a shapeless mound of white wax in it. She lit a
wooden taper from the kitchen fire, then transferred the flame from
the taper first to one candlewick and then to the other. She handed
one candlestick to me, the other to Lettie.

"Don't you have electricity?" I asked. There were electric lights
in the kitchen, big old-fashioned bulbs hanging from the ceiling,
their filaments glowing.

"Not in that part of the house," said Lettie. "The kitchen's new.
Sort of. Put your hand in front of your candle as you walk, so it
doesn't blow out."

She cupped her own hand around the flame as she said this, and
I copied her, and I walked behind her. The black kitten followed us,
out of the kitchen, through a wooden door painted white, down a
step, and into the farmhouse.

It was dark, and our candles cast huge shadows, so it looked to
me, as we walked, as if everything was moving, pushed and shaped
by the shadows, the grandfather clock and the stuffed animals and
birds (*Were* they stuffed? I wondered. Did that owl move, or was
it just the flickering candle flame that made me think that it had
turned its head as we passed?), the hall table, the chairs. All of them
moved in the candlelight, and all of them stayed perfectly still. We

went up a set of stairs, and then up some steps, and we passed an open window.

Moonlight spilled onto the stairs, brighter than our candle flames. I glanced up through the window and I saw the full moon. The cloudless sky was splashed with stars beyond all counting.

"That's the moon," I said.

"Gran likes it like that," said Lettie Hempstock.

"But it was a crescent moon yesterday. And now it's full. And it was raining. It *is* raining. But now it's not."

"Gran always likes the full moon to shine on this side of the house. She says it's restful, and it reminds her of when she was a girl," said Lettie. "And it means you don't trip on the stairs."

The kitten followed us up the stairs in a sequence of bounces. It made me smile.

At the top of the house was Lettie's room, and beside it, another room, and it was this room that we entered. A fire blazed in the hearth, illuminating the room with oranges and yellows. The room was warm and inviting. The bed had posts at each corner, and it had its own curtains. I had seen something like it in cartoons, but never in real life.

"There's clothes already set out for you to put on in the morning," said Lettie. "I'll be asleep in the room next door if you want me—just shout or knock if you need anything, and I'll come in. Gran said for you to use the inside lavatory, but it's a long way through the house, and you might get lost, so if you need to do your business there's a chamber pot under the bed, same as there's always been."

I blew out my candle, which left the room illuminated by the fire in the hearth, and I pushed through the curtains and climbed up into the bed.

The room was warm, but the sheets were cold as I got inside

them. The bed shook as something landed on it, and then small feet padded up the blankets, and a warm, furry presence pushed itself into my face and the kitten began, softly, to purr.

There was still a monster in my house, and, in a fragment of time that had, perhaps, been snipped out of reality, my father had pushed me down into the water of the bath and tried, perhaps, to drown me. I had run for miles through the dark. I had seen my father kissing and touching the thing that called itself Ursula Monkton. The dread had not left my soul.

But there was a kitten on my pillow, and it was purring in my face and vibrating gently with every purr, and, very soon, I slept.

X.

I had strange dreams in that house, that night. I woke myself in the darkness, and I knew only that a dream had scared me so badly that I had to wake up or die, and yet, try as I might, I could not remember what I had dreamed. The dream was haunting me: standing behind me, present and yet invisible, like the back of my head, simultaneously there and not there.

I missed my father and I missed my mother, and I missed my bed in my house, only a mile or so away. I missed yesterday, before Ursula Monkton, before my father's anger, before the bathtub. I wanted that yesterday back again, and I wanted it so badly.

I tried to pull the dream that had upset me so to the front of my mind, but it would not come. There had been betrayal in it, I knew, and loss, and time. The dream had left me scared to go back to sleep: the fireplace was almost dark now, with only the deep red glow of embers in the hearth to mark that it had once been burning, once had given light.

I climbed down from the four-poster bed, and felt beneath it until I found the heavy china chamber pot. I hitched up my nightgown and I used it. Then I walked to the window and looked out. The moon was still full, but now it was low in the sky, and a dark orange: what my mother called a harvest moon. But things were harvested in autumn, I knew, not in spring.

In the orange moonlight I could see an old woman—I was almost certain it was Old Mrs. Hempstock, although it was hard to see her face properly—walking up and down. She had a big long stick she was leaning on as she walked, like a staff. She reminded me of the soldiers I had seen on a trip to London, outside Buckingham Palace, as they marched backwards and forwards on parade.

I watched her, and I was comforted.

I climbed back into my bed in the dark, lay my head on the empty pillow, and thought, *I'll never go back to sleep, not now,* and then I opened my eyes and saw that it was morning.

There were clothes I had never seen before on a chair by the bed. There were two china jugs of water—one steaming hot, one cold—beside a white china bowl that I realized was a handbasin, set into a small wooden table. The fluffy black kitten had returned to the foot of the bed. It opened its eyes as I got up: they were a vivid blue-green, unnatural and odd, like the sea in summer, and it mewed a high-pitched questioning noise. I stroked it, then I got out of bed.

I mixed the hot water and the cold in the basin, and I washed my face and my hands. I cleaned my teeth with the cold water. There was no toothpaste, but there was a small round tin box on which was written *Max Melton's Remarkably Efficacious Tooth Powder,* in old-fashioned letters. I put some of the white powder on my green toothbrush, and cleaned my teeth with it. It tasted minty and lemony in my mouth.

I examined the clothes that had been left out for me. They were unlike anything I had ever worn before. There were no underpants. There was a white undershirt, with no buttons but with a long shirt-tail. There were brown trousers that stopped at the knees, a pair of long white stockings, and a chestnut-colored jacket with a V cut into the back, like a swallow's tail. The light brown socks were more like stockings. I put the clothes on as best I could, wishing there were zips or clasps, rather than hooks and buttons and stiff, unyielding buttonholes.

The shoes had silver buckles in the front, but the shoes were too big and did not fit me, so I went out of the room in my stockinged feet, and the kitten followed me.

To reach my room the night before I had walked upstairs and, at the top of the stairs, turned left. Now I turned right, and walked past Lettie's bedroom (the door was ajar, the room was empty) and made for the stairs. But the stairs were not where I remembered them. The corridor ended in a blank wall, and a window that looked out over woodland and fields.

The black kitten with the blue-green eyes mewed, loudly, as if to attract my attention, and turned back down the corridor in a self-important strut, tail held high. It led me down the hall, round a corner and down a passage I had never seen before, to a staircase. The kitten bounced amiably down the stairs, and I followed.

Ginnie Hempstock was standing at the foot of the stairs. "You slept long and well," she said. "We've already milked the cows. Your breakfast is on the table, and there's a saucer of cream by the fireplace for your friend."

"Where's Lettie, Mrs. Hempstock?"

"Off on an errand, getting stuff she may need. It has to go, the thing at your house, or there will be trouble, and worse will follow. She's already bound it once, and it slipped the bounds, so she needs to send it home."

"I just want Ursula Monkton to go away," I said. "I hate her."

Ginnie Hempstock put out a finger, ran it across my jacket. "It's not what anyone else hereabouts is wearing these days," she said. "But my mam put a little glamour on it, so it's not as if anyone will notice. You can walk around in it all you want, and not a soul will think there's anything odd about it. No shoes?"

"They didn't fit."

"I'll leave something that will fit you by the back door, then."

"Thank you."

She said, "I don't hate her. She does what she does, according to her nature. She was asleep, she woke up, she's trying to give everyone what they want."

"She hasn't given me anything I want. She says she wants to put me in the attic."

"That's as may be. You were her way here, and it's a dangerous thing to be a door." She tapped my chest, above my heart, with her forefinger. "And she was better off where she was. We would have sent her home safely—done it before for her kind a dozen times. But she's headstrong, that one. No teaching them. Right. Your breakfast is on the table. I'll be up in the nine-acre field if anyone needs me."

There was a bowl of porridge on the kitchen table and beside it, a saucer with a lump of golden honeycomb on it, and a jug of rich yellow cream.

I spooned up a lump of the honeycomb and mixed it into the thick porridge, then I poured in the cream.

There was toast, too, cooked beneath the grill as my father cooked it, with homemade blackberry jam. There was the best cup of tea I have ever drunk. By the fireplace, the kitten lapped at a saucer of creamy milk, and purred so loudly I could hear it across the room.

I wished I could purr too. I would have purred then.

Lettie came in, carrying a shopping bag, the old-fashioned kind you never seem to see anymore: elderly women used to carry them to the shops, big woven bags that were almost baskets, raffia-work out-side and lined with cloth, with rope handles. This basket was almost full. Her cheek had been scratched, and had bled, although the blood had dried. She looked miserable.

"Hello," I said.

"Well," she said. "Let me tell you, if you think that was fun, that wasn't any fun, not one bit. Mandrakes are so loud when you pull them up, and I didn't have earplugs, and once I'd got it I had to swap it for a shadow-bottle, an old-fashioned one with lots of shadows dissolved in vinegar . . ." She buttered some toast, then crushed a lump of golden honeycomb onto it and started munching. "And that was just to get me to the bazaar, and they aren't even meant to be open yet. But I got most of what I needed there."

"Can I look?"

"If you want to."

I looked into the basket. It was filled with broken toys: dolls' eyes and heads and hands, cars with no wheels, chipped cat's-eye glass marbles. Lettie reached up and took down the jam jar from the window ledge. Inside it, the silvery-translucent wormhole shifted and twisted and spiraled and turned. Lettie dropped the jam jar into the shopping bag, with the broken toys. The kitten slept, and ignored us entirely.

Lettie said, "You don't have to come with, for this bit. You can stay here while I go and talk to her."

I thought about it. "I'd feel safer with you," I told her.

She did not look happy at this. She said, "Let's go down to the ocean." The kitten opened its too-green and blue eyes and stared at us disinterestedly as we left.

There was a pair of black leather boots, like riding boots, waiting for me, by the back door. They looked old, but well cared for, and were just my size. I put them on, although I felt more comfortable in sandals. Together, Lettie and I walked down to her ocean, by which I mean, the pond.

We sat on the old bench, and looked at the placid brown surface of the pond, and the lily pads, and the scum of duckweed by the water's edge.

"You Hempstocks aren't people," I said.

"Are too."

I shook my head. "I bet you don't actually even look like that," I said. "Not really."

Lettie shrugged. "Nobody actually looks like what they really are on the inside. You don't. I don't. People are much more complicated than that. It's true of everybody."

I said, "Are you a monster? Like Ursula Monkton?"

Lettie threw a pebble into the pond. "I don't think so," she said. "Monsters come in all shapes and sizes. Some of them are things people are scared of. Some of them are things that look like things people used to be scared of a long time ago. Sometimes monsters are things people should be scared of, but they aren't."

I said, "People should be scared of Ursula Monkton."

"P'raps. What do you think Ursula Monkton is scared of?"

"Dunno. Why do you think she's scared of anything? She's a grown-up, isn't she? Grown-ups and monsters aren't scared of things."

"Oh, monsters are scared," said Lettie. "That's why they're monsters. And as for grown-ups . . ." She stopped talking, rubbed her freckled nose with a finger. Then, "I'm going to tell you something important. Grown-ups don't look like grown-ups on the inside either. Outside, they're big and thoughtless and they always know what they're doing. Inside, they look just like they always have. Like they did when they were your age. The truth is, there aren't any grown-ups. Not one, in the whole wide world." She thought for a moment. Then she smiled. "Except for Granny, of course."

We sat there, side by side, on the old wooden bench, not saying anything. I thought about adults. I wondered if that was true: if they were all really children wrapped in adult bodies, like children's books hidden in the middle of dull, long adult books, the kind with no pictures or conversations.

"I love my ocean," Lettie said, and I knew our time by the pond was done.

"It's just pretending, though," I told her, feeling like I was letting childhood down by admitting it. "Your pond. It's not an ocean. It can't be. Oceans are bigger than seas. Your pond is just a pond."

"It's as big as it needs to be," said Lettie Hempstock, nettled. She sighed. "We'd better get on with sending Ursula whatsername back where she came from." Then she said, "I do know what she's scared of. And you know what? I'm scared of them too."

The kitten was nowhere to be seen when we returned to the kitchen, although the fog-colored cat was sitting on a windowsill, staring out at the world. The breakfast things had all been tidied up and put away, and my red pajamas and my dressing gown, neatly folded, were waiting for me on the table, in a large brown-paper bag, along with my green toothbrush.

"You won't let her get me, will you?" I asked Lettie.

She shook her head, and together we walked up the winding flinty lane that led to my house and to the thing who called herself Ursula Monkton. I carried the brown-paper bag with my nightwear in it, and Lettie carried her too-big-for-her raffia shopping bag, filled with broken toys, which she had obtained in exchange for a mandrake that screamed and shadows dissolved in vinegar.

Children, as I have said, use back ways and hidden paths, while adults take roads and official paths. We went off the road, took a shortcut that Lettie knew that took us through some fields, then into the extensive abandoned gardens of a rich man's crumbling house, and then back onto the lane again. We came out just before the place where I had gone over the metal fence.

Lettie sniffed the air. "No varmints yet," she said. "That's good."

"What *are* varmints?"

She said only, "You'll know 'em when you see 'em. And I hope you'll never see 'em."

"Are we going to sneak in?"

"Why would we do that? We'll go up the drive and through the front door, like gentry."

We started up the drive. I said, "Are you going to make a spell and send her away?"

"We don't do spells," she said. She sounded a little disappointed to admit it. "We'll do recipes sometimes. But no spells or cantrips. Gran doesn't hold with none of that. She says it's *common*."

"So what's the stuff in the shopping bag for, then?"

"It's to stop things traveling when you don't want them to. Mark boundaries."

In the morning sunlight, my house looked so welcoming and so friendly, with its warm red bricks, and red tile roof. Lettie reached into the shopping bag. She took a marble from it, pushed it into the still-damp soil. Then, instead of going into the house, she turned left, walking the edge of the property. By Mr. Wollery's vegetable patch we stopped and she took something else from her shopping bag: a headless, legless, pink doll-body, with badly chewed hands. She buried it beside the pea plants.

We picked some pea pods, opened them and ate the peas inside. Peas baffled me. I could not understand why grown-ups would take things that tasted so good when they were freshly-picked and raw, and put them in tin cans, and make them revolting.

Lettie placed a toy giraffe, the small plastic kind you would find in a children's zoo, or a Noah's Ark, in the coal shed, beneath a large lump of coal. The coal shed smelled of damp and blackness and of old, crushed forests.

"Will these things make her go away?"

"No."

"Then what are they for?"

"To stop her going away."

"But we *want* her to go away."

"No. We want her to go *home*."

I stared at her: at her short brownish-red hair, her snub-nose, her freckles. She looked three or four years older than me. She might have been three or four thousand years older, or a thousand times older again. I would have trusted her to the gates of Hell and back. But still . . .

"I wish you'd explain properly," I said. "You talk in mysteries all the time."

I was not scared, though, and I could not have told you why I was not scared. I trusted Lettie, just as I had trusted her when we had gone in search of the flapping thing beneath the orange sky. I believed in her, and that meant I would come to no harm while I was with her. I knew it in the way I knew that grass was green, that roses had sharp, woody thorns, that breakfast cereal was sweet.

We went into my house through the front door. It was not locked—unless we went away on holidays I do not ever remember it being locked—and we went inside.

My sister was practicing the piano in the front room. We went in. She heard the noise, stopped playing "Chopsticks" and turned around.

She looked at me curiously. "What happened last night?" she asked. "I thought you were in trouble, but then Mummy and Daddy

came back and you were just staying with your friends. Why would
they say you were sleeping at your friends'? You don't have any
friends." She noticed Lettie Hempstock, then. "Who's this?"

"My friend," I told her. "Where's the horrible monster?"

"Don't call her that," said my sister. "She's *nice*. She's having a
lie-down."

My sister did not say anything about my strange clothes.

Lettie Hempstock took a broken xylophone from her shopping
bag and dropped it onto the scree of toys that had accumulated between the piano and the blue toy-box with the detached lid.

"There," she said. "Now it's time to go and say hello."

The first faint stirrings of fear inside my chest, inside my mind.
"Go up to her room, you mean?"

"Yup."

"What's she doing up there?"

"Doing things to people's lives," said Lettie. "Only local people
so far. She finds what they think they need and she tries to give it to
them. She's doing it to make the world into something she'll be happier in. Somewhere more comfortable for her. Somewhere cleaner.
And she doesn't care so much about giving them money, not anymore. Now what she cares about more is people hurting."

As we went up the stairs Lettie placed something on each step:
a clear glass marble with a twist of green inside it; one of the little
metal objects we called knucklebones; a bead; a pair of bright blue
doll's eyes, connected at the back with white plastic, to make them
open or close; a small red and white horseshoe magnet; a black
pebble; a badge, the kind that came attached to birthday cards, with
I Am Seven on it; a book of matches; a plastic ladybird with a black
magnet in the base; a toy car, half-squashed, its wheels gone; and, last
of all, a lead soldier. It was missing a leg.

We were at the top of the stairs. The bedroom door was closed. Lettie said, "She won't put you in the attic." Then, without knocking, she opened the door, and she went into the bedroom that had once been mine and, reluctantly, I followed.

Ursula Monkton was lying on the bed with her eyes closed. She was the first adult woman who was not my mother that I had seen naked, and I glanced at her curiously. But the room was more interesting to me than she was.

It was my old bedroom, but it wasn't. Not anymore. There was the little yellow handbasin, just my size, and the walls were still robin's-egg blue, as they had been when it was mine. But now strips of cloth hung from the ceiling, gray, ragged cloth strips, like bandages, some only a foot long, others dangling almost all the way to the floor. The window was open and the wind rustled and pushed them, so they swayed, grayly, and it seemed as if perhaps the room was moving, like a tent or a ship at sea.

"You have to go now," said Lettie.

Ursula Monkton sat up on the bed, and then she opened her eyes, which were now the same gray as the hanging cloths. She said, in a voice that still sounded half-asleep, "I wondered what I would have to do to bring you both here, and look, you came."

"You didn't bring us here," Lettie said. "We came because we wanted to. And I came to give you one last chance to go."

"I'm not going anywhere," said Ursula Monkton, and she sounded petulant, like a very small child who wanted something. "I've only just got here. I have a house, now. I have pets—his father is just the *sweetest* thing. I'm making people happy. There is nothing like me anywhere in this whole world. I was looking, just now when you came in. I'm the only one there is. They can't defend themselves. They don't know how. So this is the best place in the whole of creation."

She smiled at us both, brightly. She really was pretty, for a grown-up, but when you are seven, beauty is an abstraction, not an imperative. I wonder what I would have done if she had smiled at me like that now: whether I would have handed my mind or my heart or my identity to her for the asking, as my father did.

"You think this world's like that," said Lettie. "You think it's easy. But it en't."

"Of course it is. What are you saying? That you and your family will defend this world against me? You're the only one who ever leaves the borders of your farm—and you tried to bind me without knowing my name. Your mother wouldn't have been that foolish. I'm not scared of you, little girl."

Lettie reached deep into the shopping bag. She pulled out the jam jar with the translucent wormhole inside, and held it out.

"Here's your way back," she said. "I'm being kind, and I'm being nice. Trust me. Take it. I don't think you can get any further to home than the place we met you, with the orange sky, but that's far enough. I can't get you from there to where you came from in the first place—I asked Gran, and she says it isn't even there anymore— but once you're back we can find a place for you, somewhere similar. Somewhere you'll be happy. Somewhere you'll be safe."

Ursula Monkton got off the bed. She stood up and looked down at us. There were no lightnings wreathing her, not any longer, but she was scarier standing naked in that bedroom than she had been floating in the storm. She was an adult—no, more than an adult. She was *old*. And I have never felt more like a child.

"I'm so happy here," she said. "So very, very happy here." And then she said, almost regretfully, "You're not."

I heard a sound, a soft, raggedy, flapping sound. The gray cloths began to detach themselves from the ceiling, one by one. They fell, but not in a straight line. They fell toward us, from all over the room, as if we were magnets, pulling them toward our bodies. The first strip of gray cloth landed on the back of my left hand, and it stuck there. I reached out my right hand and grabbed it, and I pulled the cloth off: it adhered, for a moment, and as it pulled off it made a sucking sound. There was a discolored patch on the back of my left hand, where the cloth had been, and it was as red as if I had been sucking on it for a long, long time, longer and harder than I ever had in real life, and it was beaded with blood. There were pinpricks of red wetness that smeared as I touched it, and then a long bandage-cloth began to attach itself to my legs, and I moved away as a cloth landed on my face and my forehead, and another wrapped itself over my eyes, blinding me, so I pulled at the cloth on my eyes, but now another cloth circled my wrists, bound them together, and my arms were wrapped and bound to my body, and I stumbled, and fell to the floor.

If I pulled against the cloths, they hurt me.

My world was gray. I gave up, then. I lay there, and did not move, concentrated only on breathing through the space the cloth strips had left for my nose. They held me, and they felt alive.

I lay on the carpet, and I listened. There was nothing else I could do.

Ursula said, "I need the boy safe. I promised I'd keep him in the attic, so the attic it shall be. But you, little farm-girl. What shall I do with you? Something appropriate. Perhaps I ought to turn you inside out, so your heart and brains and flesh are all naked and exposed on the outside, and the skin-side's inside. Then I'll keep you wrapped up in my room here, with your eyes staring forever at the darkness inside yourself. I can do that."

"No," said Lettie. She sounded sad, I thought. "Actually, you can't. And I gave you your chance."

"You threatened me. Empty threats."

"I dunt make threats," said Lettie. "I really wanted you to have a chance." And then she said, "When you looked around the world for things like you, didn't you wonder why there weren't lots of other old things around? No, you never wondered. You were so happy it was just you here, you never stopped to think.

"Gran always calls your sort of thing *fleas*, Skarthach of the Keep. I mean, she could call you anything. I think she thinks *fleas* is funny . . . She doesn't mind your kind. She says you're harmless enough. Just a bit stupid. That's cos there are things that eat fleas, in this part of creation. *Varmints*, Gran calls them. She dunt like them at *all*. She says they're mean, and they're hard to get rid of. And they're always hungry."

"I'm not scared," said Ursula Monkton. She sounded scared. And then she said, "How did you know my name?"

"Went looking for it this morning. Went looking for other things too. Some boundary markers, to keep you from running too far, getting into more trouble. And a trail of breadcrumbs that leads straight here, to this room. Now, open the jam jar, take out the doorway, and let's send you home."

I waited for Ursula Monkton to respond, but she said nothing. There was no answer. Only the slamming of a door, and the sound of footsteps, fast and pounding, running down the stairs.

Lettie's voice was close to me, and it said, "She would have been better off staying here, and taking me up on my offer."

I felt her hands tugging at the cloths on my face. They came free with a wet, sucking sound, but they no longer felt alive, and when they came off they fell to the ground and lay there, unmoving. This time there was no blood beaded on my skin. The worst thing that had happened was that my arms and legs had gone to sleep.

Lettie helped me to my feet. She did not look happy.

"Where did she go?" I asked.

"She's followed the trail out of the house. And she's scared. Poor thing. She's so scared."

"You're scared too."

"A bit, yes. Right about now she's going to find that she's trapped inside the bounds I put down, I expect," said Lettie.

We went out of the bedroom. Where the toy soldier at the top of the stairs had been, there was now a rip. That's the best I can describe it: it was as if someone had taken a photograph of the stairs and then torn out the soldier from the photograph. There was nothing in the space where the soldier had been but a dim grayness that hurt my eyes if I looked at it too long.

"What's she scared of?"

"You heard. Varmints."

"Are you scared of varmints, Lettie?"

She hesitated, just a moment too long. Then she said simply, "Yes."

"But you aren't scared of her. Of Ursula."

"I can't be scared of her. It's just like Gran says. She's like a flea, all puffed up with pride and power and lust, like a flea bloated with blood. But she couldn't have hurt me. I've seen off dozens like her, in my time. One as come through in Cromwell's day—now there was something to talk about. He made folk lonely, that one. They'd hurt themselves just to make the loneliness stop—gouge out their eyes or jump down wells, and all the while that great lummocking thing sits in the cellar of the Duke's Head, looking like a squat toad big as a bulldog." We were at the bottom of the stairs, walking down the hall.

"How do you know where she went?"

"Oh, she couldn't have gone anywhere but the way I laid out for her." In the front room my sister was still playing "Chopsticks" on the piano.

> *Da da DUM da da*
> *da da DUM da da*
> *da da DUM da DUM da DUM da da . . .*

We walked out of the front door. "He was nasty, that one, back in Cromwell's day. But we got him out of there just before the hunger birds came."

"Hunger birds?"

"What Gran calls varmints. The cleaners."

They didn't sound bad. I knew that Ursula had been scared of them, but I wasn't. Why would you be scared of cleaners?

XI.

We caught up with Ursula Monkton on the lawn, by the rose-bushes. She was holding the jam jar with the drifting wormhole inside it. She looked strange. She tugged at the lid, and then stopped and looked up at the sky. Then she looked back to the jam jar once more.

She ran over to my beech tree, the one with the rope ladder, and she threw the jam jar as hard as she could against the trunk. If she was trying to break it, she failed. The jar simply bounced off, and landed on the moss that half-covered the tangle of roots, and lay there, undamaged.

Ursula Monkton glared at Lettie. "Why?" she said.

"You know why," said Lettie.

"Why would you let them in?" She had started to cry, and I felt uncomfortable. I did not know what to do when adults cried. It was something I had only seen twice before in my life: I had seen my grandparents cry, when my aunt had died, in hospital, and I had seen my mother cry. Adults should not weep, I knew. They did not have mothers who would comfort them.

I wondered if Ursula Monkton had ever had a mother. She had mud on her face and on her knees, and she was wailing.

I heard a sound in the distance, odd and outlandish: a low thrumming, as if someone had plucked at a taut piece of string.

"It won't be me that lets them in," said Lettie Hempstock. "They go where they wants to. They usually don't come here because there's nothing for them to eat. Now, there is."

"Send me back," said Ursula Monkton. And now I did not think she looked even faintly human. Her face was wrong, somehow: an accidental assemblage of features that simply put me in mind of a human face, like the knobbly gray whorls and lumps on the side of my beech tree, or the patterns in the wooden headboard of the bed at my grandmother's house, which, if I looked at them wrongly in the moonlight, showed me an old man with his mouth open wide, as if he were screaming.

Lettie picked up the jam jar from the green moss, and twisted the lid. "You've gone and got it stuck tight," she said. She walked over to the rock path, turned the jam jar upside down, holding it at the bottom, and banged it, lid-side-down, once, confidently, against the ground. Then she turned it the right side up, and twisted. This time the lid came off in her hand.

She passed the jam jar to Ursula Monkton, who reached inside it, and pulled out the translucent thing that had once been a hole in my foot. It writhed and wiggled and flexed seemingly in delight at her touch.

She threw it down. It fell onto the grass, and it grew. Only it didn't grow. It *changed:* as if it was closer to me than I had thought. I could see through it, from one end to the other. I could have run down it, if the far end of that tunnel had not ended in a bitter orange sky.

As I stared at it, my chest twinged again: an ice-cold feeling, as if I had just eaten so much ice cream that I had chilled my insides.

Ursula Monkton walked toward the tunnel mouth. (How could the tiny wormhole be a tunnel? I could not understand it. It was still a glistening translucent silver-black wormhole, on the grass, no more than a foot or so long. It was as if I had zoomed in on something small, I suppose. But it was also a tunnel, and you could have taken a house through it.)

Then she stopped, and she wailed.

She said, "The way back." Only that. "Incomplete," she said. "It's broken. The last of the gate isn't there . . ." And she looked around her, troubled and puzzled. She focused on me—not my face, but my chest. And she smiled.

Then she *shook*. One moment she was an adult woman, naked and muddy, the next, as if she was a flesh-colored umbrella, she unfurled.

And as she unfurled, she reached out, and she grabbed me, pulled me up and high off the ground, and I reached out in fear and held her in my turn.

I was holding flesh. I was fifteen feet or more above the ground, as high as a tree.

I was not holding flesh.

I was holding old fabric, a perished, rotting canvas, and, beneath it, I could feel wood. Not good, solid wood, but the kind of old decayed wood I'd find where trees had crumbled, the kind that always felt wet, that I could pull apart with my fingers, soft wood with tiny beetles in it and woodlice, all filled with threadlike fungus.

It creaked and swayed as it held me.

YOU HAVE BLOCKED THE WAYS, it said to Lettie Hempstock.

"I never blocked nothing," Lettie said. "You've got my friend. Put him down." She was a long way beneath me, and I was scared of heights and I was scared of the creature that was holding me.

THE PATH IS INCOMPLETE. THE WAYS ARE BLOCKED.

"Put him down. Now. Safely."

HE COMPLETES THE PATH. THE PATH IS INSIDE
HIM.

I was certain that I would die, then.

I did not want to die. My parents had told me that I would not
really die, not the real me: that nobody really died, when they died;
that my kitten and the opal miner had just taken new bodies and
would be back again, soon enough. I did not know if this was true or
not. I knew only that I was used to being me, and I liked my books
and my grandparents and Lettie Hempstock, and that death would
take all these things from me.

I WILL OPEN HIM. THE WAY IS BROKEN. IT RE-
MAINS INSIDE HIM.

I would have kicked, but there was nothing to kick against. I
pulled with my fingers at the limb holding me, but my fingernails
dug into rotting cloth and soft wood, and beneath it, something as
hard as bone; and the creature held me close.

"Let me go!" I shouted. "Let! Me! Go!"

NO.

"Mummy!" I shouted. "Daddy!" Then, "Lettie, make her put
me down."

My parents were not there. Lettie was. She said, "Skarthach. Put
him down. I gave you a choice, before. Sending you home will be
harder, with the end of your tunnel inside him. But we can do it—
and Gran can do it if Mum and me can't. So put him down."

IT IS INSIDE HIM. IT IS NOT A TUNNEL. NOT ANY
LONGER. IT DOES NOT END. I FASTENED THE PATH
INSIDE HIM TOO WELL WHEN I MADE IT AND THE
LAST OF IT IS STILL INSIDE HIM. NO MATTER. ALL I
NEED TO DO TO GET AWAY FROM HERE IS TO REACH
INTO HIS CHEST AND PULL OUT HIS BEATING HEART
AND FINISH THE PATH AND OPEN THE DOOR.

It was talking without words, the faceless flapping thing, talking directly inside my head, and yet there was something in its words that reminded me of Ursula Monkton's pretty, musical voice. I knew it meant what it said.

"All of your chances are used up," said Lettie, as if she were telling us that the sky was blue. And she raised two fingers to her lips and, shrill and sweet and piercing sharp, she whistled.

They came as if they had been waiting for her call.

High in the sky they were, and black, jet-black, so black it seemed as if they were specks on my eyes, not real things at all. They had wings, but they were not birds. They were older than birds, and they flew in circles and in loops and whorls, dozens of them, hundreds perhaps, and each flapping unbird slowly, ever so slowly, descended.

I found myself imagining a valley filled with dinosaurs, millions of years ago, who had died in battle, or of disease: imagining first the carcasses of the rotting thunder-lizards, bigger than buses, and then the vultures of that aeon: gray-black, naked, winged but featherless; faces from nightmares—beak-like snouts filled with needle-sharp teeth, made for rending and tearing and devouring, and hungry red eyes. These creatures would have descended on the corpses of the great thunder-lizards and left nothing but bones.

Huge, they were, and sleek, and ancient, and it hurt my eyes to look at them.

"Now," said Lettie Hempstock to Ursula Monkton. "Put him down."

The thing that held me made no move to drop me. It said nothing, just moved swiftly, like a raggedy tall ship, across the grass toward the tunnel.

I could see the anger in Lettie Hempstock's face, her fists clenched so tightly the knuckles were white. I could see above us the hunger birds circling, circling . . .

And then one of them dropped from the sky, dropped faster than the mind could imagine. I felt a rush of air beside me, saw a black, black jaw filled with needles and eyes that burned like gas jets, and I heard a ripping noise, like a curtain being torn apart.

The flying thing swooped back up into the sky with a length of gray cloth between its jaws.

I heard a voice wailing inside my head and out of it, and the voice was Ursula Monkton's.

They descended, then, as if they had all been waiting for the first of their number to move. They fell from the sky onto the thing that held me, nightmares tearing at a nightmare, pulling off strips of fabric, and through it all I heard Ursula Monkton crying.

I ONLY GAVE THEM WHAT THEY NEEDED, she was saying, petulant and afraid. I MADE THEM HAPPY.

"You made my daddy hurt me," I said, as the thing that was holding me flailed at the nightmares that tore at its fabric. The hunger birds ripped at it, each bird silently tearing away strips of cloth and flapping heavily back into the sky, to wheel and descend again.

I NEVER MADE ANY OF THEM DO ANYTHING, it told me. For a moment I thought it was laughing at me, then the laughter became a scream, so loud it hurt my ears and my mind.

It was as if the wind left the tattered sails then, and the thing that was holding me crumpled slowly to the ground.

I hit the grass hard, skinning my knees and the palms of my hands. Lettie pulled me up, helped me away from the fallen, crumpled remains of what had once called itself Ursula Monkton.

There was still gray cloth, but it was not cloth: it writhed and rolled on the ground around me, blown by no wind that I could perceive, a squirming maggoty mess.

The hunger birds landed on it like seagulls on a beach of stranded fish, and they tore at it as if they had not eaten for a thousand years and needed to stuff themselves now, as it might be another thousand years or longer before they would eat again. They tore at the gray stuff and in my mind I could hear it screaming the whole time as they crammed its rotting-canvas flesh into their sharp maws.

Lettie held my arm. She didn't say anything.

We waited.

And when the screaming stopped, I knew that Ursula Monkton was gone forever.

Once the black creatures had finished devouring the thing on the grass, and nothing remained, not even the tiniest scrap of gray cloth, then they turned their attentions to the translucent tunnel, which wiggled and wriggled and twitched like a living thing. Several of them grasped it in their claws, and they flew up with it, pulling it into the sky while the rest of them tore at it, demolishing it with their hungry mouths.

I thought that when they finished it they would go away, return to wherever they had come from, but they did not. They descended. I tried to count them, as they landed, and I failed. I had thought that there were hundreds of them, but I might have been wrong. There might have been twenty of them. There might have been a thousand. I could not explain it: perhaps they were from a place where such things as counting didn't apply, somewhere outside of time and numbers.

They landed, and I stared at them, but saw nothing but shadows.

So many shadows.

And they were staring at us.

Lettie said, "You've done what you came here for. You got your prey. You cleaned up. You can go home now."

The shadows did not move.

She said, "Go!"

The shadows on the grass stayed exactly where they were. If anything they seemed darker, more real than they had been before.

— *You have no power over us.*

"Perhaps I don't," said Lettie. "But I called you here, and now I'm telling you to go home. You devoured Skarthach of the Keep. You've done your business. Now clear off."

— *We are cleaners. We came to clean.*

"Yes, and you've cleaned the thing you came for. Go home."

— *Not everything,* sighed the wind in the rhododendron bushes and the rustle of the grass.

Lettie turned to me, and put her arms around me. "Come on," she said. "Quickly."

We walked across the lawn, rapidly. "I'm taking you down to the fairy ring," she said. "You have to wait there until I come and get you. Don't leave. Not for anything."

"Why not?"

"Because something bad could happen to you. I don't think I could get you back to the farmhouse safely, and I can't fix this on my own. But you're safe in the ring. Whatever you see, whatever you hear, don't leave it. Just stay where you are and you'll be fine."

"It's not a real fairy ring," I told her. "That's just our games. It's a green circle of grass."

"It is what it is," she said. "Nothing that wants to hurt you can cross it. Now, stay inside." She squeezed my hand, and walked me into the green grass circle. Then she ran off, into the rhododendron bushes, and she was gone.

XII.

The shadows began to gather around the edges of the circle. Formless blotches that were only there, really there, when glimpsed from the corners of my eyes. That was when they looked birdlike. That was when they looked hungry.

I have never been as frightened as I was in that grass circle with the dead tree in the center, on that afternoon. No birds sang, no insects hummed or buzzed. Nothing changed. I heard the rustle of the leaves and the sigh of the grass as the wind passed over it, but Lettie Hempstock was not there, and I heard no voices in the breeze. There was nothing to scare me but shadows, and the shadows were not even properly visible when I looked at them directly.

The sun got lower in the sky, and the shadows blurred into the dusk, became, if anything, more indistinct, so now I was not certain that anything was there at all. But I did not leave the grass circle.

"Hey! Boy!"

I turned. He walked across the lawn toward me. He was dressed as he had been the last time I had seen him: a dinner jacket, a frilly white shirt, a black bow-tie. His face was still an alarming cherry-red, as if he had just spent too long on the beach, but his hands were white. He looked like a waxwork, not a person, something you would expect to see in the Chamber of Horrors. He grinned when he saw me looking at him, and now he looked like a waxwork that was smiling, and I swallowed, and wished that the sun was out again.

"Come on, boy," said the opal miner. "You're just prolonging the inevitable."

I did not say a word. I watched him. His shiny black shoes walked up to the grass circle, but they did not cross it.

My heart was pounding so hard in my chest I was certain that he must have heard it. My neck and scalp prickled.

"Boy," he said, in his sharp South African accent. "They need to finish this up. It's what they do: they're the carrion kind, the vultures of the void. Their job. Clean up the last remnants of the mess. Nice and neat. Pull you from the world and it will be as if you never existed. Just go with it. It won't hurt."

I stared at him. Adults only ever said that when it, whatever it happened to be, was going to hurt so much.

The dead man in the dinner jacket turned his head slowly, until his face was looking at mine. His eyes were rolled back in his head, and seemed to be staring blindly at the sky above us, like a sleepwalker.

"She can't save you, your little friend," he said. "Your fate was sealed and decided days ago, when their prey used you as a door from its place to this one, and she fastened her path in your heart."

"I didn't start it!" I told the dead man. "It's not fair. *You* started it."

"Yes," said the dead man. "Are you coming?"

I sat down with my back to the dead tree in the center of the fairy ring, and I closed my eyes, and I did not move. I remembered poems to distract myself, recited them silently under my breath, mouthing the words but making no sound.

Fury said to a mouse that he met in the house let us both go to law I will prosecute you . . .

I had learned that poem by heart at my school. It was told by the Mouse from *Alice in Wonderland*, the Mouse she met swimming in the pool of her own tears. In my copy of *Alice* the words of the poem curled and shrank like a mouse's tail.

I could say all of the poem in one long breath, and I did, all the way to the inevitable end.

I'll be judge I'll be jury said cunning old Fury I'll try the whole cause and condemn you to death.

When I opened my eyes and looked up the opal miner was no longer there.

The sky was going gray and the world was losing depth and flattening into twilight. If the shadows were still there I could no longer perceive them; or rather, the whole world had become shadows.

My little sister ran down from the house, calling my name. She stopped before she reached me, and she said, "What are you doing?"

"Nothing."

"Daddy's on the phone. He says you have to come and talk to him."

"No. He doesn't."

"What?"

"He doesn't say that."

"If you don't come now, you'll be in trouble."

I did not know if this was my sister or not, but I was on the inside of the grass circle, and she was on the outside.

I wished I had brought a book with me, even though it was almost too dark to read. I said the Mouse's "Pool of Tears" poem again, in my head. *Come I'll take no denial we must have a trial for really this morning I've nothing to do . . .*

"Where's Ursula?" asked my sister. "She went up to her room, but she isn't there anymore. She's not in the kitchen and she's not in the loo-lahs. I want my tea. I'm hungry."

"You can make yourself something to eat," I told her. "You're not a baby."

"Where's Ursula?"

She was ripped to shreds by alien vulture-monsters and honestly I think you're one of them or being controlled by them or something.

"Don't know."

"I'm telling Mummy and Daddy when they get home that you were horrible to me today. You'll get into trouble." I wondered if this was actually my sister or not. It definitely sounded like her. But she did not take a step over the circle of greener grass, into the ring. She stuck her tongue out at me, and ran back toward the house.

Said the mouse to the cur such a trial dear sir with no jury or judge would be wasting our breath . . .

Deep twilit dusk, all colorless and strained. Mosquitoes whined about my ears and landed, one by one, on my cheeks and my hands. I was glad I was wearing Lettie Hempstock's cousin's strange old-fashioned clothing, then, because I had less bare skin exposed. I slapped at the insects as they landed, and some of them flew off. One that didn't fly away, gorging itself on the inside of my wrist, burst when I hit it, leaving a smeared teardrop of my blood to run down the inside of my arm.

There were bats flying above me. I liked bats, always had, but that night there were so many of them, and they made me think of the hunger birds, and I shuddered.

Twilight became, imperceptibly, night, and now I was sitting in a circle that I could no longer see, at the bottom of the garden. Lights, friendly electric lights, went on in the house.

I did not want to be scared of the dark. I was not scared of any real thing. I just did not want to be there any longer, waiting in the darkness for my friend who had run away from me and did not seem to be coming back.

. . . said cunning old Fury I'll try the whole cause and condemn you to death.

I stayed just where I was. I had seen Ursula Monkton torn to shreds, and the shreds devoured by scavengers from outside the universe of things that I understood. If I went out of the circle, I was certain, they would do the same to me.

I moved from Lewis Carroll to Gilbert and Sullivan.

When you're lying awake with a dismal headache and repose is taboo'd by anxiety, I conceive you may use any language you choose to indulge in without impropriety . . .

I loved the sound of the words, even if I was not entirely sure what all of them meant.

I needed to wee. I turned my back on the house, took a few steps away from the tree, scared I would take one step too far and find myself outside the circle. I urinated into the darkness. I had just finished when I was blinded by a torch beam, and my father's voice said, "What on earth are you doing down here?"

"1 . . . I'm just down here," I said.

"Yes. Your sister said. Well, time to come back to the house. Your dinner's on the table."

I stayed where I was. "No," I said, and shook my head.

"Don't be silly."

"I'm not being silly. I'm staying here."

"Come on." And then, more cheerful, "Come on, Handsome George." It had been his silly pet name for me, when I was a baby. He even had a song that went with it that he would sing while bouncing me on his lap. It was the best song in the world.

I didn't say anything.

"I'm not going to carry you back to the house," said my father. There was an edge starting to creep into his voice. "You're too big for that."

Yes, I thought. *And you'd have to cross into the fairy ring to pick me up.*

But the fairy ring seemed foolish now. This was my father, not some waxwork thing that the hunger birds had made to lure me out. It was night. My father had come home from work. It was time.

I said, "Ursula Monkton's gone away. And she's not ever coming back."

He sounded irritated, then. "What did you do? Did you say something horrible to her? Were you rude?"

"No."

He shone the torch beam onto my face. The light was almost blinding. He seemed to be fighting to keep his temper under control. He said, "Tell me what you said to her."

"I didn't say anything to her. She just went away."

It was true, or almost.

"Come back to the house, now."

"Please, Daddy. I have to stay here."

"You come back to the house this minute!" shouted my father, at the top of his voice, and I could not help it: my lower lip shook, my nose started to run, and tears sprang to my eyes. The tears blurred my vision and stung, but they did not fall, and I blinked them away.

I did not know if I was talking to my own father or not.

I said, "I don't like it when you shout at me."

"Well, I don't like it when you act like a little animal!" he shouted, and now I was crying, and the tears were running down my face, and I wished that I was anywhere else but there that night.

I had stood up to worse things than him in the last few hours. And suddenly, I didn't care anymore. I looked up at the dark shape behind and above the torch beam, and I said, "Does it make you feel big to make a little boy cry?" and I knew as I said it that it was the thing I should never have said.

His face, what I could see of it in the reflected torchlight, crumpled, and looked shocked. He opened his mouth to speak, then he closed it again. I could not remember my father ever at a loss for words, before or after. Only then. I felt terrible. I thought, *I will die here soon. I do not want to die with those words on my lips.*

But the torch beam was turning away from me. My father said only, "We'll be up at the house. I'll put your dinner in the oven."

I watched the torchlight move back across the lawn, past the rosebushes and up toward the house, until it went out, and was lost to sight. I heard the back door open and close again.

Then you get some repose in the form of a doze with hot eyeballs and head ever aching but your slumbering teems with such horrible dreams that you'd very much better be waking . . .

Somebody laughed. I stopped singing, and looked around, but saw nobody.

"'The Nightmare Song,'" a voice said. "How appropriate."

She walked closer, until I could see her face. Ursula Monkton was still quite naked, and she was smiling. I had seen her torn to pieces a few hours before, but now she was whole. Even so, she looked less solid than any of the other people I had seen that night; I could see the lights of the house glimmering behind her, through her. Her smile had not changed.

"You're dead," I told her.

"Yes. I was eaten," said Ursula Monkton.

"You're dead. You aren't real."

"I was eaten," she repeated. "I am nothing. And they have let me out, just for a little while, from the place inside them. It's cold in there, and very empty. But they have promised you to me, so I will have something to play with; something to keep me company in the dark. And after you have been eaten, you too will be nothing. But whatever remains of that nothing will be mine to keep, eaten and together, my toy and my distraction, until the end of time. We'll have such *fun*."

A ghost of a hand was raised, and it touched the smile, and it blew me the ghost of Ursula Monkton's kiss.

"I'll be waiting for you," she said.

A rustle in the rhododendrons behind me and a voice, cheerful and female and young, saying, "It's okay. Gran fixed it. Everything's taken care of. Come on."

The moon was visible now above the azalea bush, a bright crescent like a thick nail paring.

I sat down by the dead tree, and did not move.

"Come on, silly. I told you. They've gone home," said Lettie Hempstock.

"If you're really Lettie Hempstock," I told her, "you come here."

She stayed where she was, a shadowy girl. Then she laughed, and she stretched and she shook, and now she was only another shadow: a shadow that filled the night.

"You are hungry," said the voice in the night, and it was no longer Lettie's voice, not any longer. It might have been the voice inside my own head, but it was speaking aloud. "You are tired. Your family hates you. You have no friends. And Lettie Hempstock, I regret to tell you, is never coming back."

I wished I could have seen who was talking. If you have something specific and visible to fear, rather than something that could be anything, it is easier.

"Nobody cares," said the voice, so resigned, so practical. "Now, step out of the circle and come to us. One step is all it will take. Just put one foot across the threshold and we will make all the pain go away forever: the pain you feel now and the pain that is still to come. It will never happen."

It was not one voice, not any longer. It was two people talking in unison. Or a hundred people. I could not tell. So many voices.

"How can you be happy in this world? You have a hole in your heart. You have a gateway inside you to lands beyond the world you know. They will call you, as you grow. There can never be a time when you forget them, when you are not, in your heart, questing after something you cannot have, something you cannot even properly imagine, the lack of which will spoil your sleep and your day and your life, until you close your eyes for the final time, until your loved ones give you poison and sell you to *anatomy*, and even then you will die with a hole inside you, and you will wail and curse at a life ill-lived. But you won't grow. You can come out, and we will end it, cleanly, or you can die in there, of hunger and of fear. And when you are dead your circle will mean nothing, and we will tear out your heart and take your soul for a keepsake."

"P'raps it will be like that," I said, to the darkness and the shadows, "and p'raps it won't. And p'raps if it is, it would have been like that anyway. I don't care. I'm still going to wait here for Lettie Hempstock, and she's going to come back to me. And if I die here, then I still die waiting for her, and that's a better way to go than you and all you stupid horrible things tearing me to bits because I've got something inside me that I don't even *want*!"

There was silence. The shadows seemed to have become part of the night once again. I thought over what I'd said, and I knew that it was true. At that moment, for once in my childhood, I was not scared of the dark, and I *was* perfectly willing to die (as willing as any seven-year-old, certain of his immortality, can be) if I died waiting for Lettie. Because she was my friend.

Time passed. I waited for the night to begin to talk to me again, for people to come, for all the ghosts and monsters of my imagination to stand beyond the circle and call me out, but nothing more happened. Not then. I simply waited.

The moon rose higher. My eyes had adjusted to the darkness. I sang, under my breath, mouthing the words over and over.

> You're a regular wreck with a crick in your neck
> and no wonder you snore for your head's on the floor
> and you've needles and pins from your sole to your shins
> and your flesh is a-creep for your left leg's asleep
> and you've cramp in your toes and a fly on your nose
> you've got fluff in your lung and a feverish tongue
> and a thirst that's intense and a general sense that you haven't been
> sleeping in clover . . .

I sang it to myself, the whole song, all the way through, two or three times, and I was relieved that I remembered the words, even if I did not always understand them.

XIII.

When Lettie arrived, the real Lettie, this time, she was carrying a bucket of water. It must have been heavy judging from the way she carried it. She stepped over where the edge of the ring in the grass must have been and she came straight to me.

"Sorry," she said. "That took a lot longer than I expected. It didn't want to cooperate, neither, and in the end it took me and Gran to do it, and she did most of the heavy lifting. It wasn't going to argue with her, but it didn't help, and it's not easy—"

"What?" I asked. "What are you talking about?"

She put the metal bucket down on the grass beside me without spilling a drop. "The ocean," she said. "It didn't want to go. It gave Gran such a struggle that she said she was going to have to go and have a lie-down afterwards. But we still got it into the bucket in the end."

The water in the bucket was glowing, emitting a greenish-blue light. I could see Lettie's face by it. I could see the waves and ripples on the surface of the water, watch them crest and splash against the side of the bucket.

"I don't understand."

"I couldn't get you to the ocean," she said. "But there was nothing stopping me bringing the ocean to you."

I said, "I'm hungry, Lettie. And I don't like this."

"Mum's made dinner. But you're going to have to stay hungry for a little bit longer. Were you scared, up here on your own?"

"Yes."

"Did they try and get you out of the circle?"

"Yes."

She took my hands in hers, then, and squeezed them. "But you stayed where you were meant to be, and you didn't listen to them. Well done. That's quality, that is." And she sounded proud. In that moment I forgot my hunger and I forgot my fear.

"What do I do now?" I asked her.

"Now," she said, "you step into the bucket. You don't have to take your shoes off or anything. Just step in."

It did not even seem a strange request. She let go of one of my hands, kept hold of the other. I thought, *I will never let go of your hand, not unless you tell me to*. I put one foot into the glimmering water of the bucket, raising the water level almost to the edge. My foot rested on the tin floor of the bucket. The water was cool on my foot, not cold. I put the other foot into the water and I went down with it, down like a marble statue, and the waves of Lettie Hempstock's ocean closed over my head.

I felt the same shock you would feel if you had stepped backwards, without looking, and had fallen into a swimming pool. I closed my eyes at the water's sting and kept them tightly shut, so tightly.

I could not swim. I did not know where I was, or what was happening, but even under the water I could feel that Lettie was still holding my hand.

I was holding my breath.

I held it until I could hold it no longer, and then I let the air out in a bubbling rush and gulped a breath in, expecting to choke, to splutter, to die.

I did not choke. I felt the coldness of the water—if it was

water—pour into my nose and my throat, felt it fill my lungs, but that was all it did. It did not hurt me.

I thought, *This is the kind of water you can breathe.* I thought, *Perhaps there is just a secret to breathing water, something simple that everyone could do, if only they knew.* That was what I thought.

That was the first thing I thought.

The second thing I thought was that I knew everything. Lettie Hempstock's ocean flowed inside me, and it filled the entire universe, from Egg to Rose. I knew that. I knew what Egg was—where the universe began, to the sound of uncreated voices singing in the void—and I knew where Rose was—the peculiar crinkling of space on space into dimensions that fold like origami and blossom like strange orchids, and which would mark the last good time before the eventual end of everything and the next Big Bang, which would be, I knew now, nothing of the kind.

I knew that Old Mrs. Hempstock would be here for that one, as she had been for the last.

I saw the world I had walked since my birth and I understood how fragile it was, that the reality I knew was a thin layer of icing on a great dark birthday cake writhing with grubs and nightmares and hunger. I saw the world from above and below. I saw that there were patterns and gates and paths beyond the real. I saw all these things and understood them and they filled me, just as the waters of the ocean filled me.

Everything whispered inside me. Everything spoke to everything, and I knew it all.

I opened my eyes, curious to learn what I would see in the world outside me, if it would be anything like the world inside.

I was hanging deep beneath the water.

I looked down, and the blue world below me receded into darkness. I looked up and the world above me did the same. Nothing was pulling me down deeper, nothing was forcing me toward the surface.

I turned my head, a little, to look at her, because she was still holding my hand, she had never let go of my hand, and I saw Lettie Hempstock.

At first, I do not think I knew what I was looking at. I could make no sense of it. Where Ursula Monkton had been made of gray cloth that flapped and snapped and gusted in the storm-winds, Lettie Hempstock was made of silken sheets the color of ice, filled with tiny flickering candle flames, a hundred hundred candle flames.

Could there be candle flames burning under the water? There could. I knew that, when I was in the ocean, and I even knew how. I understood it just as I understood Dark Matter, the material of the universe that makes up everything that must be there but we cannot find. I found myself thinking of an ocean running beneath the whole universe, like the dark seawater that laps beneath the wooden boards of an old pier: an ocean that stretches from forever to forever and is still small enough to fit inside a bucket, if you have Old Mrs. Hempstock to help you get it in there, and you ask nicely.

Lettie Hempstock looked like pale silk and candle flames. I wondered how I looked to her, in that place, and knew that even in a place that was nothing but knowledge that was the one thing I could not know. That if I looked inward I would see only infinite mirrors, staring into myself for eternity.

The silk filled with candle flames moved then, a slow, graceful, under-the-water sort of a movement. The current pulled at it, and now it had arms and the hand that had never let go of mine, and a body and a freckled face that was familiar, and it opened its mouth and, in Lettie Hempstock's voice, it said, "I'm really sorry."

"What for?"

She did not reply. The currents of the ocean pulled at my hair and my clothes like summer breezes. I was no longer cold and I knew everything and I was not hungry and the whole big, complicated world was simple and graspable and easy to unlock. I would stay here for the rest of time in the ocean which was the universe which was the soul which was all that mattered. I would stay here forever.

"You can't," said Lettie. "It would destroy you."

I opened my mouth to tell her that nothing could kill me, not now, but she said, "Not kill you. Destroy you. Dissolve you. You wouldn't die in here, nothing ever dies in here, but if you stayed here for too long, after a while just a little of you would exist everywhere, all spread out. And that's not a good thing. Never enough of you all together in one place, so there wouldn't be anything left that would think of itself as an 'I.' No point of view any longer, because you'd be an infinite sequence of views and of points . . ."

I was going to argue with her. She was wrong, she had to be: I loved that place, that state, that feeling, and I was never going to leave it.

And then my head broke water, and I blinked and coughed, and I was standing, thigh-deep in the pond at the back of the Hempstocks' farm, and Lettie Hempstock was standing beside me, holding my hand.

I coughed again, and it felt like the water fled my nose, my throat, my lungs. I pulled clean air into my chest, in the light of the huge, full harvest moon, that shone on the Hempstocks' red-tiled roof, and, for one final, perfect moment, I still knew everything: I remember that I knew how to make it so the moon would be full when you needed it to be, and shining just on the back of the house, every night.

I knew everything, but Lettie Hempstock was pulling me up out of the pond.

I was still wearing the strange old-fashioned clothes I had been given that morning, and as I stepped out of the pond, up onto the grass that edged it, I discovered that my clothes and my skin were now perfectly dry. The ocean was back in the pond, and the only knowledge I was left with, as if I had woken from a dream on a summer's day, was that it had not been long ago since I had known everything.

I looked at Lettie in the moonlight. "Is that how it is for you?" I asked.

"Is *what* how it is for me?"

"Do you still know everything, all the time?"

She shook her head. She didn't smile. She said, "Be boring, knowing everything. You have to give all that stuff up if you're going to muck about here."

"So you *used* to know everything?"

She wrinkled her nose. "Everybody did. I told you. It's nothing special, knowing how things work. And you really do have to give it all up if you want to play."

"To play *what*?"

"This," she said. She waved at the house and the sky and the impossible full moon and the skeins and shawls and clusters of bright stars.

I wished I knew what she meant. It was as if she was talking about a dream we had shared. For a moment it was so close in my mind that I could almost touch it.

"You must be so hungry," said Lettie, and the moment was broken, and yes, I was so hungry, and the hunger took my head and swallowed my lingering dreams.

There was a plate waiting for me in my place at the table in the farmhouse's huge kitchen. On it was a portion of shepherd's pie, the mashed potato a crusty brown on top, minced meat and vegetables and gravy beneath it. I was scared of eating food outside my home, scared that I might want to leave food I did not like and be told off, or be forced to sit and swallow it in minuscule portions until it was gone, as I was at school, but the food at the Hempstocks' was always perfect. It did not scare me.

Ginnie Hempstock was there, bustling about in her apron, rounded and welcoming. I ate without talking, head down, shoveling the welcome food into my mouth. The woman and the girl spoke in low, urgent tones.

"They'll be here soon enough," said Lettie. "They aren't stupid. And they won't leave until they've taken the last little bit of what they came here for."

Her mother sniffed. Her red cheeks were flushed from the heat of the kitchen fire. "Stuff and nonsense," she said. "They're all mouth, they are."

I had never heard that expression before, and I thought she was telling us that the creatures were just mouths and nothing more. It did not seem unlikely that the shadows were indeed all mouths. I had seen them devour the gray thing that had called itself Ursula Monkton.

My grandmother would tell me off for eating like a wild animal. "You must *essen*, eat," she would say, "like a person, not a *chazzer*, a pig. When animals eat, they *fress*. People *essen*. Eat like a person." *Fressen*: that was how the hunger birds had taken Ursula Monkton and it was also, I had no doubt, how they would consume me.

"I've never seen so many of them," said Lettie. "When they came here in the old days there was only a handful of them."

Ginnie poured me a glass of water. "That's your own fault," she told Lettie. "You put up signals, and called them. Like banging the dinner bell, you were. Not surprising they all came."

"I just wanted to make sure that *she* left," said Lettie.

"Fleas," said Ginnie, and she shook her head. "They're like chickens who get out of the henhouse, and are so proud of themselves and so puffed up for being able to eat all the worms and beetles and caterpillars they want, that they never think about foxes." She stirred the custard cooking on the hob, with a long wooden spoon in huge, irritated movements. "Anyway, now we've got foxes. And we'll send them all home, same as we did the last times they were sniffing around. We did it before, didn't we?"

"Not really," said Lettie. "Either we sent the flea home, and the varmints had nothing to hang around for, like the flea in the cellar in Cromwell's time, or the varmints came and took what they came here for and then they went away. Like the fat flea who made people's dreams come true in Red Rufus's day. They took him and they upped and left. We've never had to get rid of them before."

Her mother shrugged. "It's all the same sort of thing. We'll just send them back where they came from."

"And where *do* they come from?" asked Lettie.

I had slowed down now, and was making the final fragments of my shepherd's pie last as long as I could, pushing them around the plate slowly with my fork.

"That dunt matter," said Ginnie. "They all go back eventually. Probably just get bored of waiting."

"I tried pushing them around," said Lettie Hempstock, matter-of-factly. "Couldn't get any traction. I held them with a dome of protection, but that wouldn't have lasted much longer. We're good here, obviously—nothing's coming into this farm without our say-so."

"In *or* out," said Ginnie. She removed my empty plate, replaced it with a bowl containing a steaming slice of spotted dick with thick yellow custard drizzled all over it.

I ate it with joy.

I do not miss childhood, but I miss the way I took pleasure in small things, even as greater things crumbled. I could not control the world I was in, could not walk away from things or people or moments that hurt, but I found joy in the things that made me happy. The custard was sweet and creamy in my mouth, the dark swollen currants in the spotted dick were tangy in the cake-thick chewy blandness of the pudding, and perhaps I was going to die that night and perhaps I would never go home again, but it was a good dinner, and I had faith in Lettie Hempstock.

The world outside the kitchen was still waiting. The Hempstocks' fog-colored house cat—I do not believe I ever knew her name—padded through the kitchen. That reminded me . . .

"Mrs. Hempstock? Is the kitten still here? The black one with the white ear?"

"Not tonight," said Ginnie Hempstock. "She's out and about. She was asleep on the chair in the hall all this afternoon."

I wished I could stroke her soft fur. I wanted, I realized, to say goodbye.

"Um. I suppose. If I *do*. Have to die. Tonight," I started, haltingly, not sure where I was going. I was going to ask for something, I imagine—for them to say goodbye to my mummy and daddy, or to tell my sister that it wasn't fair that nothing bad ever happened to her: that her life was charmed and safe and protected, while I was forever stumbling into disaster. But nothing seemed right, and I was relieved when Ginnie interrupted me.

"Nobody is going to die tonight," said Ginnie Hempstock, firmly. She took my empty bowl and washed it out in the sink, then she dried her hands on her apron. She took the apron off, went out into the hallway and returned a few moments later wearing a plain brown coat and a pair of large dark green Wellington boots.

Lettie seemed less confident than Ginnie. But Lettie, with all her age and wisdom, was a girl, while Ginnie was an adult, and her confidence reassured me. I had faith in them both.

"Where's Old Mrs. Hempstock?" I asked.

"Having a lie-down," said Ginnie. "She's not as young as she used to be."

"How old *is* she?" I asked, not expecting to get an answer. Ginnie just smiled, and Lettie shrugged.

I held Lettie's hand as we left the farmhouse, promising myself that this time I would not let it go.

XIV.

When I had entered the farmhouse, through the back door, the moon had been full, and it was a perfect summer's night. When I left, I went with Lettie Hempstock and her mother out of the front door, and the moon was a thin white smile, high in a cloudy sky, and the night was gusty with sudden, undecided spring breezes coming first from one direction, then from another; every now and again a gust of wind would contain a sprinkling of rain that never amounted to anything more than that.

We walked through the manure-stinking farmyard and up the lane. We passed a bend in the road, and we stopped. Although it was dark, I knew exactly where I was. This was where it had all begun. It was the corner where the opal miner had parked my family's white Mini, the place that he had died all alone, with a face the color of pomegranate juice, aching for his lost money, on the edge of the Hempstock land where the barriers between life and death were thin.

I said, "I think we should wake up Old Mrs. Hempstock."

"It doesn't work like that," said Lettie. "When she gets tired, she sleeps until she wakes up on her own. A few minutes or a hundred years. There's no waking her. Might as well try and wake up an atom bomb."

Ginnie Hempstock planted herself in the middle of the lane, facing away from the farmhouse.

"Right!" she shouted to the night. "Let's be having you."

Nothing. A wet wind that gusted and was gone.

Lettie said, "P'raps they've all gone home . . . ?"

"Be nice if they had," said Ginnie. "All this palaver and non-sense."

I felt guilty. It was, I knew, my fault. If I had kept hold of Lettie's hand none of this would have happened. Ursula Monkton, the hunger birds, these things were undoubtedly my responsibility. Even what had happened—or now, had, perhaps, no longer happened—in the cold bath, the previous night.

I had a thought.

"Can't you just snip it out? The thing in my heart, that they want? Maybe you could snip it out like your granny snipped things last night?"

Lettie squeezed my hand in the dark.

"Maybe Gran could do that if she was here," she said. "I can't. I don't think Mum can either. It's really hard, snipping things out of time: you have to make sure that the edges all line up, and even Gran doesn't always get it right. And this would be harder than that. It's a real thing. I don't think even Gran could take it out of you without hurting your heart. And you need your heart." Then she said, "They're coming."

But I knew something was happening, knew it before she said anything. For the second time I saw the ground begin to glow golden; I watched the trees and the grass, the hedgerows and the willow clumps and the last stray daffodils begin to shine with a burnished half-light. I looked around, half-fearful, half with wonder, and I observed that the light was brightest behind the house and over to the west, where the pond was.

I heard the beating of mighty wings, and a series of low thumps.

I turned and I saw them: the vultures of the void, the carrion kind, the hunger birds.

They were not shadows any longer, not here, not in this place. They were all-too-real, and they landed in the darkness, just beyond the golden glow of the ground. They landed in the air and in trees, and they shuffled forward, as close as they could get to the golden ground of the Hempstocks' farm. They were huge—each of them was much bigger than I was.

I would have been hard-pressed to describe their faces, though. I could see them, look at them, take in every feature, but the moment I looked away they were gone, and there was nothing in my mind where the hunger birds had been but tearing beaks and talons, or wriggling tentacles, or hairy, chitinous mandibles. I could not keep their true faces in my head. When I turned away the only knowledge I retained was that they had been looking directly at me, and that they were ravenous.

"Right, my proud beauties," said Ginnie Hempstock, loudly. Her hands were on the hips of her brown coat. "You can't stay here. You know that. Time to get a move on." And then she said simply, "Hop it."

They shifted but they did not move, the innumerable hunger birds, and began to make a noise. I thought that they were whispering amongst themselves, and then it seemed to me that the noise they were making was an amused chuckle.

I heard their voices, distinct but twining together, so I could not tell which creature was speaking.

— *We are hunger birds. We have devoured palaces and worlds and kings and stars. We can stay wherever we wish to stay.*

— *We perform our function.*

— *We are necessary.*

And they laughed so loudly it sounded like a train approaching. I squeezed Lettie's hand, and she squeezed mine.

— *Give us the boy.*

Ginnie said, "You're wasting your time, and you're wasting mine. Go home."

— *We were summoned here. We do not need to leave until we have done what we came here for. We restore things to the way they are meant to be. Will you deprive us of our function?*

"Course I will," said Ginnie. "You've had your dinner. Now you're just making nuisances of yourselves. Be off with you. Blinking varmints. I wouldn't give tuppence ha'penny for the lot of you. Go home!" And she shook her hand in a flicking gesture.

One of the creatures let out a long, wailing scream of appetite and frustration.

Lettie's hold on my hand was firm. She said, "He's under our protection. He's on our land. And one step onto our land and that's the end of you. So go away."

The creatures seemed to huddle closer. There was silence in the Sussex night: only the rustle of leaves in the wind, only the call of a distant owl, only the sigh of the breeze as it passed; but in that silence I could hear the hunger birds conferring, weighing up their options, plotting their course. And in that silence I felt their eyes upon me.

Something in a tree flapped its huge wings and cried out, a shriek that mingled triumph and delight, an affirmative shout of hunger and joy. I felt something in my heart react to the scream, like the tiniest splinter of ice inside my chest.

— *We cannot cross the border. This is true. We cannot take the child from your land. This also is true. We cannot hurt your farm or your creatures . . .*

"That's right. You can't. So get along with you! Go home. Haven't you got a war to be getting back to?"

— *We cannot hurt your world, true.*

— *But we can hurt this one.*

One of the hunger birds reached a sharp beak down to the ground at its feet, and began to tear at it—not as a creature that eats earth and grass, but as if it were eating a curtain or a piece of scenery with the world painted on it. Where it devoured the grass, nothing remained—a perfect nothing, only a color that reminded me of gray, but a formless, pulsing gray like the shifting static of our television screen when you dislodged the aerial cord and the picture had gone completely.

This was the void. Not blackness, not nothingness. This was what lay beneath the thinly painted scrim of reality.

And the hunger birds began to flap and to flock.

They landed on a huge oak tree and they tore at it and they wolfed it down, and in moments the tree was gone, along with everything that had been behind it.

A fox slipped out of a hedgerow and slunk down the lane, its eyes and mask and brush illuminated golden by the farm-light. Before it had made it halfway across the road it had been ripped from the world, and there was only void behind it.

Lettie said, "What he said before. We have to wake Gran."

"She won't like that," said Ginnie. "Might as well try and wake a—"

"Dunt matter. If we can't wake her up, they'll destroy the whole of this creation."

Ginnie said only, "I don't know *how.*"

A clump of hunger birds flew up to a patch of the night sky where stars could be seen through the breaks in the clouds, and they tore at a kite-shaped constellation I could never have named, and they scratched and they rent and they gulped and they swallowed. In a handful of heartbeats, where the constellation and sky had been, there was now only a pulsing nothingness that hurt my eyes if I looked at it directly.

I was a normal child. Which is to say, I was selfish and I was not entirely convinced of the existence of things that were not me, and I was certain, rock-solid unshakably certain, that I was the most important thing in creation. There was nothing that was more important to me than I was.

Even so, I understood what I was seeing. The hunger birds would—no, they *were*—ripping the world away, tearing it into nothing. Soon enough, there would be no world. My mother, my father, my sister, my house, my school friends, my town, my grandparents, London, the Natural History Museum, France, television, books, ancient Egypt—because of me, all these things would be gone, and there would be nothing in their place.

I did not want to die. More than that, I did not want to die as Ursula Monkton had died, beneath the rending talons and beaks of things that may not even have had legs or faces.

I did not want to die at all. Understand that.

But I could not let everything be destroyed, when I had it in my power to stop the destruction.

I let go of Lettie Hempstock's hand and I ran, as fast as I could, knowing that to hesitate, even to slow down, would be to change my mind, which would be the worst thing that I could do, which would be to save my life.

How far did I run? Not far, I suppose, as these things go.

Lettie Hempstock was shouting at me to stop, but still, I ran, crossing the farmland, where every blade of grass, every pebble on the lane, every willow tree and hazel hedge glowed golden, and I ran toward the darkness beyond the Hempstock land. I ran and I hated myself for running, as I had hated myself the time I had jumped from the high board at the swimming pool. I knew there was no going back, that there was no way that this could end in anything but pain, and I knew that I was willing to exchange my life for the world.

They took off into the air, the hunger birds, as I ran toward them, as pigeons will rise when you run at them. They wheeled and they circled, deep shadows in the dark.

I stood there in the darkness and I waited for them to descend. I waited for their beaks to tear at my chest, and for them to devour my heart.

I stood there for perhaps two heartbeats, and it felt like forever.

It happened.

Something slammed into me from behind and knocked me down into the mud on the side of the lane, face-first. I saw bursts of light that were not there. The ground hit my stomach, and the wind was knocked out of me.

(*A ghost-memory rises, here: a phantom moment, a shaky reflection in the pool of remembrance. I know how it would have felt when the scavengers took my heart. How it felt as the hunger birds, all mouth, tore into my chest and snatched out my heart, still pumping, and devoured it to get at what was hidden inside it. I know how that feels, as if it was truly a part of my life, of my death. And then the memory snips and rips, neatly, and——*)

A voice said, "Idiot! Don't move. Just don't," and the voice was Lettie Hempstock's, and I could not have moved if I had wanted to. She was on top of me, and she was heavier than I was, and she was pushing me down, face-first, into the grass and the wet earth, and I could see nothing.

I felt them, though.

I felt them crash into her. She was holding me down, making herself a barrier between me and the world.

I heard Lettie's voice wail in pain.

I felt her shudder and twitch.

There were ugly cries of triumph and hunger, and I could hear my own voice whimpering and sobbing, so loud in my ears . . .

A voice said, "This is unacceptable."

It was a familiar voice, but still, I could not place it, or move to see who was talking.

Lettie was on top of me, still shaking, but as the voice spoke, she stopped moving. The voice continued, "On what authority do you harm my child?"

A pause. Then,

— *She was between us and our lawful prey.*

"You're scavengers. Eaters of offal, of rubbish, of garbage. You're cleaners. Do you think that you can harm my family?"

I knew who was talking. The voice sounded like Lettie's gran, like Old Mrs. Hempstock. Like her, I knew, and yet so unlike. If Old Mrs. Hempstock had been an empress, she might have talked like that, her voice more stilted and formal and yet more musical than the old-lady voice I knew.

Something wet and warm was soaking my back.

— *No . . . No, lady.*

That was the first time I heard fear or doubt in the voice of one of the hunger birds.

"There are pacts, and there are laws and there are treaties, and you have violated all of them."

Silence then, and it was louder than words could have been. They had nothing to say.

I felt Lettie's body being rolled off mine, and I looked up to see Ginnie Hempstock's sensible face. She sat on the ground on the edge of the road, and I buried my face in her bosom. She took me in one arm, and her daughter in the other.

From the shadows, a hunger bird spoke, with a voice that was not a voice, and it said only,

— *We are sorry for your loss.*

"Sorry?" The word was spat, not said.

Ginnie Hempstock swayed from side to side, crooning low and wordlessly to me and to her daughter. Her arms were around me. I lifted my head and I looked back at the person speaking, my vision blurred by tears.

I stared at her.

It was Old Mrs. Hempstock, I suppose. But it wasn't. It was Lettie's gran in the same way that . . .

I mean . . .

She shone silver. Her hair was still long, still white, but now she stood as tall and as straight as a teenager. My eyes had become too used to the darkness, and I could not look at her face to see if it was the face I was familiar with: it was too bright. Magnesium-flare bright. Fireworks Night bright. Midday-sun-reflecting-off-a-silver-coin bright.

I looked at her as long as I could bear to look, and then I turned my head, screwing my eyes tightly shut, unable to see anything but a pulsating afterimage.

The voice that was like Old Mrs. Hempstock's said, "Shall I bind you creatures in the heart of a dark star, to feel your pain in a place where every fragment of a moment lasts a thousand years? Shall I invoke the compacts of Creation, and have you all removed from the list of created things, so there never will have been any hunger birds, and anything that wishes to traipse from world to world can do it with impunity?"

I listened for a reply, but heard nothing. Only a whimper, a mewl of pain or of frustration.

"I'm done with you. I will deal with you in my own time and in my own way. For now I must tend to the children."

— *Yes, lady.*

— *Thank you, lady.*

"Not so fast. Nobody's going anywhere before you put all those things back like they was. There's Boötes missing from the sky. There's an oak tree gone, and a fox. You put them all back, the way they were." And then the silvery empress voice added, in a voice that was now also unmistakably Old Mrs. Hempstock's, *"Varmints."*

Somebody was humming a tune. I realized, as if from a long way away, that it was me, at the same moment that I remembered what the tune was: "Girls and Boys Come Out to Play."

> . . . *the moon doth shine as bright as day.*
> *Leave your supper and leave your meat,*
> *and join your playfellows in the street.*
> *Come with a whoop and come with a call.*
> *Come with a whole heart or not at all . . .*

I held on to Ginnie Hempstock. She smelled like a farm and like a kitchen, like animals and like food. She smelled very real, and the realness was what I needed at that moment.

I reached out a hand, tentatively touched Lettie's shoulder. She did not move or respond.

Ginnie started speaking, then, but at first I did not know if she was talking to herself or to Lettie or to me. "They overstepped their bounds," she said. "They could have hurt you, child, and it would have meant nothing. They could have hurt this world without anything being said—it's only a world, after all, and they're just sand grains in the desert, worlds. But Lettie's a Hempstock. She's outside of their dominion, my little one. And they hurted her."

I looked at Lettie. Her head had flopped down, hiding her face. Her eyes were closed.

"Is she going to be all right?" I asked.

Ginnie didn't reply, just hugged us both the tighter to her bosom, and rocked, and crooned a wordless song.

The farm and its land no longer glowed golden. I could not feel anything in the shadows watching me, not any longer.

"Don't you worry," said an old voice, now familiar once more. "You're safe as houses. Safer'n most houses I've seen. They've gone."

"They'll come back again," I said. "They want my heart."

"They'd not come back to this world again for all the tea in China," said Old Mrs. Hempstock. "Not that they've got any use for tea—or for China—no more than a carrion crow does."

Why had I thought her dressed in silver? She wore a much-patched gray dressing gown over what had to have been a nightie, but a nightie of a kind that had not been fashionable for several hundred years.

The old woman put a hand on her granddaughter's pale forehead, lifted it up, then let it go.

Lettie's mother shook her head. "It's over," she said.

I understood it then, at the last, and felt foolish for not understanding it sooner. The girl beside me, on her mother's lap, at her mother's breast, had given her life for mine.

"They were meant to hurt me, not her," I said.

"No reason they should've taken either of you," said the old lady, with a sniff. I felt guilt then, guilt beyond anything I had ever felt before.

"We should get her to hospital," I said, hopefully. "We can call a doctor. Maybe they can make her better."

Ginnie shook her head.

"Is she dead?" I asked.

"Dead?" repeated the old woman in the dressing gown. She sounded offended. "Has hif," she said, grandly aspirating each aitch as if that were the only way to convey the gravity of her words to me. "Has hif han 'Empstock would hever do hanything so . . . *common* . . ."

"She's hurt," said Ginnie Hempstock, cuddling me close. "Hurt as badly as she *can* be hurt. She's so close to death as makes no odds if we don't do something about it, and quickly." A final hug, then, "Off with you, now." I clambered reluctantly from her lap, and I stood up.

Ginnie Hempstock got to her feet, her daughter's body limp in her arms. Lettie lolled and was jogged like a rag doll as her mother got up, and I stared at her, shocked beyond measure.

I said, "It was my fault. I'm sorry. I'm really sorry."

Old Mrs. Hempstock said, "You meant well," but Ginnie Hempstock said nothing at all. She walked down the lane toward the farm, and then she turned off behind the milking shed. I thought that Lettie was too big to be carried, but Ginnie carried her as if she weighed no more than a kitten, her head and upper body resting on Ginnie's shoulder, like a sleeping infant being taken upstairs to bed. Ginnie carried her down that path, and beside the hedge, and back, and back, until we reached the pond.

There were no breezes back there, and the night was perfectly still; our path was lit by moonlight and nothing more; the pond, when we got there, was just a pond. No golden, glimmering light. No magical full moon. It was black and dull, with the moon, the true moon, the quarter moon, reflected in it.

I stopped at the edge of the pond, and Old Mrs. Hempstock stopped beside me.

But Ginnie Hempstock kept walking.

She staggered down into the pond, until she was wading thigh-deep, her coat and skirt floating on the water as she waded, breaking the reflected moon into dozens of tiny moons that scattered and re-formed around her.

At the center of the pond, with the black water above her hips, she stopped. She took Lettie from her shoulder, so the girl's body was supported at the head and at the knees by Ginnie Hempstock's practical hands; then slowly, so very slowly, she laid Lettie down in the water.

The girl's body floated on the surface of the pond.

Ginnie took a step back, and then another, never looking away from her daughter.

I heard a rushing noise, as if of an enormous wind coming toward us.

Lettie's body shook.

There was no breeze, but now there were whitecaps on the surface of the pond. I saw waves, gentle, lapping waves at first, and then bigger waves that broke and slapped at the edge of the pond. One wave crested and crashed down close to me, splashing my clothes and face. I could taste the water's wetness on my lips, and it was salt.

I whispered, "I'm sorry, Lettie."

I should have been able to see the other side of the pond. I had seen it a few moments before. But the crashing waves had taken it away, and I could see nothing beyond Lettie's floating body but the vastness of the lonely ocean, and the dark.

The waves grew bigger. The water began to glow in the moonlight, as it had glowed when it was in a bucket, glowed a pale, perfect blue. The black shape on the surface of the water was the body of the girl who had saved my life.

Bony fingers rested on my shoulder. "What are you apologizing for, boy? For killing her?"

I nodded, not trusting myself to speak.

"She's not dead. You didn't kill her, nor did the hunger birds, although they did their best to get to you through her. She's been given to her ocean. One day, in its own time, the ocean will give her back."

I thought of corpses and of skeletons with pearls for eyes. I thought of mermaids with tails that flicked when they moved, like my goldfishes' tails had flicked before my goldfish had stopped moving, to lie, belly up, like Lettie, on the top of the water. I said, "Will she be the same?"

The old woman guffawed, as if I had said the funniest thing in the universe. "Nothing's ever the same," she said. "Be it a second later or a hundred years. It's always churning and roiling. And people change as much as oceans."

Ginnie clambered out of the water, and she stood at the water's edge beside me, her head bowed. The waves crashed and smacked and splashed and retreated. There was a distant rumble that became a louder and louder rumble: something was coming toward us, across the ocean. From miles away, from hundreds and hundreds of miles away it came: a thin white line etched in the glowing blue, and it grew as it approached.

The great wave came, and the world rumbled, and I looked up as it reached us: it was taller than trees, than houses, than mind or eyes could hold, or heart could follow.

Only when it reached Lettie Hempstock's floating body did the enormous wave crash down. I expected to be soaked, or, worse, to be swept away by the angry ocean water, and I raised my arm to cover my face.

There was no splash of breakers, no deafening crash, and when I lowered my arm I could see nothing but the still black water of a pond in the night, and there was nothing on the surface of the pond but a smattering of lily pads and the thoughtful, incomplete reflection of the moon.

Old Mrs. Hempstock was gone, too. I had thought that she was standing beside me, but only Ginnie stood there, next to me, staring down silently into the dark mirror of the little pond.

"Right," she said. "I'll take you home."

XV.

There was a Land Rover parked behind the cowshed. The doors were open and the ignition key was in the lock. I sat on the newspaper-covered passenger seat and watched Ginnie Hempstock turn the key. The engine sputtered a few times before it started.

I had not imagined any of the Hempstocks driving. I said, "I didn't know you had a car."

"Lots of things you don't know," said Mrs. Hempstock, tartly. Then she glanced at me more gently and said, "You can't know everything." She backed the Land Rover up and it bumped its way forward across the ruts and the puddles of the back of the farmyard.

There was something on my mind.

"Old Mrs. Hempstock says that Lettie isn't really dead," I said. "But she looked dead. I think she is actually dead. I don't think it's true that she's not dead."

Ginnie looked like she was going to say something about the nature of truth, but all she said was, "Lettie's hurt. Very badly hurt. The ocean has taken her. Honestly, I don't know if it will ever give her back. But we can hope, can't we?"

"Yes." I squeezed my hands into fists, and I hoped as hard as I knew how.

We bumped and jolted up the lane at fifteen miles per hour.

I said, "Was she—is she—really your daughter?" I didn't know,

I still don't know, why I asked her that. Perhaps I just wanted to know more about the girl who had saved my life, who had rescued me more than once. I didn't know anything about her.

"More or less," said Ginnie. "The men Hempstocks, my brothers, they went out into the world, and they had babies who've had babies. There are Hempstock women out there in your world, and I'll wager each of them is a wonder in her own way. But only Gran and me and Lettie are the pure thing."

"She didn't have a daddy?" I asked.

"No."

"Did you have a daddy?"

"You're all questions, aren't you? No, love. We never went in for that sort of thing. You only need men if you want to breed more men."

I said, "You don't have to take me home. I could stay with you. I could wait until Lettie comes back from the ocean. I could work on your farm, and carry stuff, and learn to drive a tractor."

She said, "No," but she said it kindly. "You get on with your own life. Lettie gave it to you. You just have to grow up and try and be worth it."

A flash of resentment. It's hard enough being alive, trying to survive in the world and find your place in it, to do the things you need to do to get by, without wondering if the thing you just did, whatever it was, was worth someone having . . . if not *died*, then having given up her life. It wasn't *fair*.

"Life's not fair," said Ginnie, as if I had spoken aloud.

She turned into our driveway, pulled up outside the front door. I got out and she did too.

"Better make it easier for you to go home," she said.

Mrs. Hempstock rang the doorbell, although the door was never locked, and industriously scraped the soles of her Wellington boots on the doormat until my mother opened the door. She was dressed for bed, and wearing her quilted pink dressing gown.

"Here he is," said Ginnie. "Safe and sound, the soldier back from the wars. He had a lovely time at our Lettie's going-away party, but now it's time for this young man to get his rest."

My mother looked blank—almost confused—and then the confusion was replaced by a smile, as if the world had just reconfigured itself into a form that made sense.

"Oh, you didn't have to bring him back," said my mother. "One of us would have come and picked him up." Then she looked down at me. "What do you say to Mrs. Hempstock, darling?"

I said it automatically. "Thank-you-for-having-me."

My mother said, "Very good, dear." Then, "Lettie's going away?"

"To Australia," said Ginnie. "To be with her father. We'll miss having this little fellow over to play, but, well, we'll let you know when Lettie comes back. He can come over and play, then."

I was getting tired. The party had been fun, although I could not remember much about it. I knew that I would not visit the Hempstock farm again, though. Not unless Lettie was there.

Australia was a long, long way away. I wondered how long it would be until she came back from Australia with her father. Years, I supposed. Australia was on the other side of the world, across the ocean . . .

A small part of my mind remembered an alternate pattern of events and then lost it, as if I had woken from a comfortable sleep and looked around, pulled the bedclothes over me, and returned to my dream.

Mrs. Hempstock got back into her ancient Land Rover, so bespattered with mud (I could now see, in the light above the front door) that there was almost no trace of the original paintwork visible, and she backed it up, down the drive, toward the lane.

My mother seemed unbothered that I had returned home in fancy dress clothes at almost eleven at night. She said, "I have some bad news, dear."

"What's that?"

"Ursula's had to leave. Family matters. Pressing family matters. She's already left. I know how much you children liked her."

I knew that I didn't like her, but I said nothing.

There was now nobody sleeping in my bedroom at the top of the stairs. My mother asked if I would like my room back for a while. I said no, unsure of why I was saying no. I could not remember why I disliked Ursula Monkton so much—indeed, I felt faintly guilty for disliking her so absolutely and so irrationally—but I had no desire to return to that bedroom, despite the little yellow handbasin just my size, and I remained in the shared bedroom until our family moved out of that house half a decade later (we children protesting, the adults I think just relieved that their financial difficulties were over).

The house was demolished after we moved out. I would not go and see it standing empty, and refused to witness the demolition. There was too much of my life bound up in those bricks and tiles, those drainpipes and walls.

Years later, my sister, now an adult herself, confided in me that she believed that our mother had fired Ursula Monkton (whom she remembered, so fondly, as the only nice one in a sequence of grumpy childminders) because our father was having an affair with her. It was possible, I agreed. Our parents were still alive then, and I could have asked them, but I didn't.

My father did not mention the events of those nights, not then, not later.

I finally made friends with my father when I entered my twenties. We had so little in common when I was a boy, and I am certain I had been a disappointment to him. He did not ask for a child with a book, off in its own world. He wanted a son who did what he had done: swam and boxed and played rugby, and drove cars at speed with abandon and joy, but that was not what he had wound up with.

I did not ever go down the lane all the way to the end. I did not think of the white Mini. When I thought of the opal miner, it was in context of the two rough raw opal-rocks that sat on our mantelpiece, and in my memory he always wore a checked shirt and jeans. His face and arms were tan, not the cherry-red of monoxide poisoning, and he had no bow-tie.

Monster, the ginger tomcat the opal miner had left us, had wandered off to be fed by other families, and although we saw him, from time to time, prowling the ditches and trees at the side of the lane, he would not ever come when we called. I was relieved by this, I think. He had never been our cat. We knew it, and so did he.

A story only matters, I suspect, to the extent that the people in the story change. But I was seven when all of these things happened, and I was the same person at the end of it that I was at the beginning, wasn't I? So was everyone else. They must have been. People don't change.

Some things changed, though.

A month or so after the events here, and five years before the ramshackle world I lived in was demolished and replaced by trim, squat, regular houses containing smart young people who worked in the city but lived in my town, who made money by moving money from place to place but who did not build or dig or farm or weave, and nine years before I would kiss smiling Callie Anders . . .

I came home from school. The month was May, or perhaps early

June. She was waiting by the back door as if she knew precisely where she was and who she was looking for: a young black cat, a little larger than a kitten now, with a white splodge over one ear, and with eyes of an intense and unusual greenish-blue.

She followed me into the house.

I fed her with an unused can of Monster's cat food, which I spooned into Monster's dusty cat bowl.

My parents, who had never noticed the ginger tom's disappearance, did not initially notice the arrival of the new kitten-cat, and by the time my father commented on her existence she had been living with us for several weeks, exploring the garden until I came home from school, then staying near me while I read or played. At night she would wait beneath the bed until the lights were turned out, then she would accommodate herself on the pillow beside me, grooming my hair, and purring, so quietly as never to disturb my sister.

I would fall asleep with my face pressed into her fur, while her deep electrical purr vibrated softly against my cheek.

She had such unusual eyes. They made me think of the seaside, and so I called her Ocean, and could not have told you why.

Epilogue

I sat on the dilapidated green bench beside the duck pond, in the back of the red-brick farmhouse, and I thought about my kitten.

I only remembered that Ocean had grown into a cat, and that I had adored her for years. I wondered what had happened to her, and then I thought, *It doesn't matter that I can't remember the details any longer: death happened to her. Death happens to all of us.*

A door opened in the farmhouse, and I heard feet on the path. Soon the old woman sat down beside me. "I brung you a cup of tea," she said. "And a cheese and tomato sandwich. You've been out here for quite a while. I thought you'd probably fallen in."

"I sort of did," I told her. And, "Thank you." It had become dusk, without my noticing, while I had been sitting there.

I took the tea, and sipped it, and I looked at the woman, more carefully this time. I compared her to my memories of forty years ago. I said, "You aren't Lettie's mother. You're her grandmother, aren't you? You're Old Mrs. Hempstock."

"That's right," she said, unperturbed. "Eat your sandwich."

I took a bite of my sandwich. It was good, really good. Freshly baked bread, sharp, salty cheese, the kind of tomatoes that actually taste like something.

I was awash in memory, and I wanted to know what it meant. I said, "Is it true?" and felt foolish. Of all the questions I could have asked, I had asked that.

Old Mrs. Hempstock shrugged. "What you remembered? Probably. More or less. Different people remember things differently, and you'll not get any two people to remember anything the same, whether they were there or not. You stand two of you lot next to each other, and you could be continents away for all it means anything."

There was another question I needed answered. I said, "Why did I come here?"

She looked at me as if it were a trick question. "The funeral," she said. "You wanted to get away from everyone and be on your own. So first of all you drove back to the place you'd lived in as a boy, and when that didn't give you what you missed, you drove to the end of the lane and you came here, like you always do."

"Like I always do?" I drank some more tea. It was still hot, and strong enough: a perfect cup of builder's tea. *You could stand a spoon straight up in it,* as my father always said of a cup of tea of which he approved.

"Like you always do," she repeated.

"No," I said. "You're wrong. I mean, I haven't been here since, well, since Lettie went to Australia. Her going-away party." And then I said, "Which never happened. You know what I mean."

"You come back, sometimes," she said. "You were here once when you were twenty-four, I remember. You had two young children, and you were so scared. You came here before you left this part of the world: you were, what, in your thirties, then? I fed you a good meal in the kitchen, and you told me about your dreams and the art you were making."

"I don't remember."

She pushed the hair from her eyes. "It's easier that way."

I sipped my tea, and finished the sandwich. The mug was white, and so was the plate. The endless summer evening was coming to an end.

I asked her again, "Why did I come here?"

"Lettie wanted you to," said somebody.

The person who said that was walking around the pond: a woman in a brown coat, wearing Wellington boots. I looked at her in confusion. She looked younger than I was now. I remembered her as vast, as adult, but now I saw she was only in her late thirties. I remembered her as stout, but she was buxom, and attractive in an apple-cheeked sort of a way. She was still Ginnie Hempstock, Lettie's mother, and she looked, I was certain, just as she had looked forty-something years ago.

She sat down on the bench on the other side of me, so I was flanked by Hempstock women. She said, "I think Lettie just wants to know if it was worth it."

"If what was worth it?"

"You," said the old woman, tartly.

"Lettie did a very big thing for you," said Ginnie. "I think she mostly wants to find out what happened next, and whether it was worth everything she did."

"She . . . sacrificed herself for me."

"After a fashion, dear," said Ginnie. "The hunger birds tore out your heart. You screamed so piteously as you died. She couldn't abide that. She had to do something."

I tried to remember this. I said, "That isn't how I remember it." I thought about my heart, then; wondered if there was a cold fragment of a doorway inside it still, and if it was a gift or a curse if there was.

The old lady sniffed. "Didn't I just say you'll never get any two people to remember anything the same?" she asked.

"Can I talk to her? To Lettie?"

"She's sleeping," said Lettie's mother. "She's healing. She's not talking yet."

"Not until she's all done with where she is," said Lettie's grandmother, gesturing, but I could not tell if she was pointing to the duck pond or to the sky.

"When will that be?"

"When she's good and ready," said the old woman, as her daughter said, "Soon."

"Well," I said. "If she brought me here to look at me, let her look at me," and even as I said it I knew that it had already happened. How long had I been sitting on that bench, staring into the pond? As I had been remembering her, she had been examining me. "Oh. She did already, didn't she?"

"Yes, dear."

"And did I pass?"

The face of the old woman on my right was unreadable in the gathering dusk. On my left the younger woman said, "You don't pass or fail at being a person, dear."

I put the empty cup and plate down on the ground.

Ginnie Hempstock said, "I think you're doing better than you were the last time we saw you. You're growing a new heart, for a start."

In my memory she was a mountain, this woman, and I had sobbed and shivered on her bosom. Now she was smaller than I was, and I could not imagine her comforting me, not in that way.

The moon was full, in the sky above the pond. I could not for the life of me remember what phase the moon had been in the last time I had noticed it. I could not actually remember the last time I had done more than glance at the moon.

"So what will happen now?"

"Same thing as happens every other time you've come here," said the old woman. "You go home."

"I don't know where that is, anymore," I told them.

"You always say that," said Ginnie.

In my head Lettie Hempstock was still a full head taller than I was. She was eleven, after all. I wondered what I would see—who I would see—if she stood before me now.

The moon in the duck pond was full as well, and I found myself, unbidden, thinking of the holy fools in the old story, the ones who had gone fishing in a lake for the moon, with nets, convinced that the reflection in the water was nearer and easier to catch than the globe that hung in the sky.

And, of course, it always is.

I got up and walked a few steps to the edge of the pond. "Lettie," I said, aloud, trying to ignore the two women behind me. "Thank you for saving my life."

"She should never've taken you with her in the first place, when she went off to find the start of it all," sniffed Old Mrs. Hempstock. "Nothing to stop her sorting it all out on her own. Didn't need to take you along for company, silly thing. Well, that'll learn her for next time."

I turned and looked at Old Mrs. Hempstock. "Do you really remember when the moon was made?" I asked.

"I remember lots of things," she said.

"Will I come back here again?" I asked.

"That's not for you to know," said the old woman.

"Get along now," said Ginnie Hempstock, gently. "There's people who are wondering where you've got to."

And when she mentioned them, I realized, with an awkward horror, that my sister, her husband, her children, all the well-wishers and mourners and visitors would be puzzling over what had become of me. Still, if there was a day that they would find my absent ways easy to forgive, it was today.

It had been a long day and a hard one. I was glad that it was over. I said, "I hope that I haven't been a bother."

"No, dear," said the old woman. "No bother at all."

I heard a cat meow. A moment later, it sauntered out of the shadows and into a patch of bright moonlight. It approached me confidently, pushed its head against my shoe.

I crouched beside it and scratched its forehead, stroked its back. It was a beautiful cat, black, or so I imagined, the moonlight having swallowed the color of things. It had a white spot over one ear.

I said, "I used to have a cat like this. I called her Ocean. She was beautiful. I don't actually remember what happened to her."

"You brought her back to us," said Ginnie Hempstock. She touched my shoulder with her hand, squeezing it for a heartbeat; she touched my cheek with her fingertips, as if I were a small child, or a lover, and then she walked away, back into the night.

I picked up my plate and my mug, and I carried them along the path with me as we made our way back to the house, the old woman and I.

"The moon does shine as bright as day," I said. "Like in the song."

"It's good to have a full moon," she agreed.

I said, "It's funny. For a moment, I thought there were two of you. Isn't that odd?"

"It's just me," said the old woman. "It's only ever just me."

"I know," I said. "Of course it is."

I was going to take the plate and mug into the kitchen and put them in the sink, but she stopped me at the farmhouse door. "You ought to get back to your family now," she said. "They'll be sending out a search party."

"They'll forgive me," I said. I hoped that they would. My sister would be concerned, and there would be people I barely knew disappointed not to have told me how very, very sorry they were for my loss. "You've been so kind. Letting me sit and think, here. By the pond. I'm very grateful."

"Stuff and nonsense," she said. "Nothing kind about it."

"Next time Lettie writes from Australia," I said, "please tell her I said hello."

"I will," she said. "She'll be glad you thought of her."

I got into the car and started the engine. The old woman stood in the doorway, watching me, politely, until I had turned the car around and was on my way back up the lane.

I looked back at the farmhouse in my rearview mirror, and a trick of the light made it seem as if two moons hung in the sky above it, like a pair of eyes watching me from above: one moon perfectly full and round, the other, its twin on the other side of the sky, a half-moon.

Curiously I turned in my seat and looked back: a single half-moon hung over the farmhouse, peaceful and pale and perfect.

I wondered where the illusion of the second moon had come from, but I only wondered for a moment, and then I dismissed it from my thoughts. Perhaps it was an afterimage, I decided, or a ghost: something that had stirred in my mind, for a moment, so powerfully that I believed it to be real, but now was gone, and faded into the past like a memory forgotten, or a shadow into the dusk.

ACKNOWLEDGMENTS

This book is the book you have just read. It's done. Now we're in the acknowledgments. This is not really part of the book. You do not have to read it. It's mostly just names.

I owe thanks to so many people, the ones who were there in my life when I needed them, the ones who brought me tea, the ones who wrote the books that brought me up. To single any of them out is foolish, but here I go . . .

When I finished this book, I sent it to many of my friends to read, and they read it with wise eyes and they told me what worked for them and what needed work. I'm grateful to all of them, but particular thanks must go to Maria Dahvana Headley, Olga Nunes, Alina Simone (queen of titles), Gary K. Wolfe, Kat Howard, Kelly McCullough, Eric Sussman, Hayley Campbell, Valya Dudycz Lupescu, Melissa Marr, Elyse Marshall, Anthony Martignetti, Peter Straub, Kat Dennings, Gene Wolfe, Gwenda Bond, Anne Bobby, Lee "Budgie" Barnett, Morris Shamah, Farah Mendelsohn, Henry Selick, Clare Coney, Grace Monk, and Cornelia Funke.

This novel began, although I did not know it was going to be a novel at the time, when Jonathan Strahan asked me to write him a short story. I started to tell the story of the opal miner and the Hempstock family (who have lived in the farm in my head for such a long time), and Jonathan was forgiving and kind when I finally admitted to myself and to him that this wasn't a short story, and I let it become a novel instead.

The family in this book is not my own family, who have been gracious in letting me plunder the landscape of my own childhood and watched as I liberally reshaped those places into a story. I'm grateful to them all, especially to my youngest sister, Lizzy, who encouraged me and sent me long-forgotten memory-jogging photographs. (I wish I'd remembered the old greenhouse in time to put it into the book.)

In Sarasota, Florida, Stephen King reminded me of the joy of just writing every day. Words save our lives, sometimes.

Tori gave me a safe house to write it in, and I cannot thank her enough.

Art Spiegelman gave me his kind permission to use a word balloon from his collaborative conversation with Maurice Sendak in *The New Yorker* as the opening epigraph.

As this book entered its second draft, as I was typing out my handwritten first draft, I would read the day's work to my wife, Amanda, at night in bed, and I learned more about the words I'd written when reading them aloud to her than I ever have learned about anything I've done. She was the book's first reader, and her puzzlement and occasional frustration, her questions and her delight were my guides through subsequent drafts. I wrote this book for Amanda, when she was far away and I missed her very much. My life would be grayer and duller without her.

My daughters, Holly and Maddy, and my son, Michael, were my wisest and gentlest critics of all.

I have wonderful editors on both sides of the Atlantic: Jennifer Brehl and Jane Morpeth, and Rosemary Brosnan, who all read the book in first draft and all suggested different things I needed to change and fix and rebuild. Jane and Jennifer have also both coped extremely well with the arrival of a book that none of us was expecting, not even me.

I would very much like to thank the committee for the Zena Sutherland Lectures, held at the Chicago Public Library: the Zena Sutherland Lecture I delivered in 2012 was, in retrospect, mostly a conversation with myself about this book while I was writing it, to try and understand what I was writing and who it was for.

Merrilee Heifetz has been my literary agent for twenty-five years now. Her support on this book, as with everything over the last quarter of a century, was invaluable. Jon Levin, my agent for films and such, is a fine reader and does a mean Ringo Starr impression.

The good folk of Twitter were extremely helpful when I needed to double-check how much blackjacks and fruit salad sweets cost in the 1960s. Without them I might have written my book twice as fast.

And lastly, my thanks to the Hempstock family, who, in one form or another, have always been there when I needed them.

Neil Gaiman,
Isle of Skye,
July 2012